THE SECRET OF THE FORGOTTEN CITY

Gold! There are rumors that long ago a treasure was hidden in a city now buried under the Nevada desert.

Nancy and her friends plan to join a dig sponsored by two colleges to hunt for the gold. Before she starts, the young sleuth receives an ancient stone tablet with petroglyphs on it. With this amazing clue, however, come a threat and danger from a thief who also wants the treasure.

One harrowing adventure after another besets Nancy, Bess, George, Ned, Burt, and Dave in 102-degree temperatures as they pursue Nancy's hunches above and below ground. They are assisted by a fine Indian woman and a young geology student, but both are unwilling participants in a strange plot.

In the end Nancy and Ned nearly lose their lives, just after she has discovered the priceless hidden treasure of gold.

"Perhaps I can translate what these men are saying,"
Nancy said.

NANCY DREW MYSTERY STORIES

The Secret
of the
Forgotten City

BY CAROLYN KEENE

PUBLISHERS *Grosset & Dunlap* NEW YORK

Contents

The Secret
of the
Forgotten City

CHAPTER I

Fleetfoot Joe

"Au! Au! Au!" cried Ned Nickerson, as he eased himself out of his car and hurried toward the open front door of the Drew home.

Nancy, who was waiting for him, leaped to his side. "Ned, what happened? You're hurt!"

The tall dark-haired athlete burst into laughter and kissed her. "No hurts at all. I didn't say *'Ouch, ouch, ouch!'* I said, 'Au! Au! Au!' "

"What does that mean?" asked the attractive strawberry blond, as she led him indoors. "Please stop talking in riddles."

The couple sat down on the living-room couch. "Well?" Nancy prompted.

"Au refers to a treasure buried deep underground," Ned replied. "Want to help find it?"

"Of course," Nancy said, excited at the thought of a mystery. "Where is it and what is it?"

1

Ned grinned. "I'll give you a hint. Think of some chemistry symbols."

At once Nancy guessed the answer. "How stupid of me not to have thought of gold. *Au* is the symbol for it. Tell me where and what this treasure is."

"Not until everyone gets here," Ned replied.

"Everyone? Who is everyone?" Nancy asked.

Ned's eyes twinkled. "First there were two. Then there were four. Now we number six."

"You're being exasperating," Nancy said. "Shall I guess again?"

When he nodded, she mentioned her closest friends, Bess Marvin and George Fayne, who were cousins. The three girls lived in River Heights and had been friends for years. Then she named two boys who were fraternity brothers of Ned's at Emerson College.

"Right," Ned replied. "Your Dad, who, by the way, is enthusiastic about your recovering this gold, invited them here to dinner tonight. Your kind housekeeper, Hannah Gruen, knows the secret and is preparing my favorite dish."

"Which is—hot-pepper salad," Nancy teased. "But tell me, why all the secrecy? It's not my birthday!"

Ned answered with a grin. "We wanted to see if we could keep our plan a secret from the world's most famous girl detective."

Nancy blushed, but before she had a chance

to answer, she and Ned heard shouting out in the street.

Ned leaped to a front window. Nancy, glancing out of a side window, saw a man dashing down the long Drew driveway toward the rear of the property.

A woman's large handbag swung from one hand!

"Quick, Ned!" Nancy shouted. "Follow me!"

As the couple dashed through the kitchen, she called to the startled housekeeper, "Hannah, run out the front door. I think a woman on the sidewalk has just been robbed!"

Nancy and Ned rushed from the kitchen door in time to observe the thief pausing at the thick hedge that separated the Drews' yard from the property at the rear. Seeing the couple, he pushed his way through the bushes, since they were too high for him to vault.

"Nancy, run to the side street," Ned suggested. "If that man tries to escape that way, yell and I'll come running."

As Ned finished speaking, he was halfway through the hedge. Nancy ran back of the garage to the side street. She looked up and down the pavement, then into the yard. Suddenly the thief dashed out from behind a neighbor's house toward a car whose motor was running. A man sat at the wheel.

"Stop!" Nancy cried out. When the suspect

kept going, she ordered, "Drop that handbag!"

The stranger did neither, but just as he reached the car, Ned leaped toward him. The man tossed the bag at Nancy with a vicious thrust and jumped into the car. It roared off. Ned had missed him, and Nancy had had to move aside to avoid being hit by the car.

Her mind, however, had recorded a good image of the suspected thief. He was five feet ten, rather large-boned, had tanned, tightly drawn skin, black eyes, and shiny black hair.

"Part Indian," Nancy told herself, as she picked up the handbag and was joined by Ned.

"Too bad that fellow got away," he commented. "I memorized the license number." He repeated it to Nancy. "The man should be easy to trace."

Nancy and Ned walked to the front lawn to find out what Hannah had learned. An odd picture met their eyes. A short, stout Indian woman, about fifty years old, sat on the ground with her legs crossed under her. She was staring into space, oblivious of Hannah Gruen, who was trying to comfort her.

The Indian kept murmuring, "Nancy Drew, Nancy Drew!"

As the girl appeared, holding the handbag, she said kindly, "Here is your bag, and I am Nancy Drew."

The woman looked up, took her property, and

A woman's large handbag swung from the thief's hand.

without speaking opened the bag. An expression of dismay crossed her face and she uttered an involuntary "Oh!"

"Is something missing?" Nancy asked.

"Records. My ancestors' records."

Then the woman thought of something. She unzipped a pocket in the lining of the bag and drew out a thin stone slab about five by seven inches, on which several crude figures and symbols had been chiseled.

"These are petroglyphs and very old," the woman explained. "There were six other tablets in the bag. I planned to bring only this one, but I didn't want to leave the others unguarded in my house, so I brought them."

Hannah Gruen spoke. "I think we should all go into the house and talk."

"And call the police," Nancy added. "I'll do that immediately. Oh, by the way, what is your name and address?" she asked the Indian.

"Mrs. Wabash. My home is in Nevada, but I am staying at the River View Motel across town. I walked over here."

As Mrs. Wabash rose, with Ned helping her, Nancy hurried into the house to phone police headquarters. By the time she had given all the pertinent facts to the sergeant on duty, the other three walked inside. Everyone sat down in the living room except Hannah, who went to get cool drinks and pieces of nut-covered sponge cake for the guests.

Mrs. Wabash apologized profusely for all the trouble she had caused, and thanked Nancy and Ned sincerely for recovering her handbag and at least one of the stone tablets.

"I'm sure the thief will be caught soon," Nancy assured her. "Anyway, what could he do with the records?"

The Indian woman sipped the drink Hannah had served. "I'm not sure," she said. "I have studied ancient stones with petroglyphs—that's picture-carving on stone—and made a sort of dictionary of their meanings. The only copy I had was in my handbag."

There was a pause, then Nancy said, "It's a shame the pages were taken. Had you translated the history of your family or of any tribe?"

"It is still a puzzle as to what the history is, but I've done the best I could," Mrs. Wabash replied. "Many symbols could have two or more interpretations. For instance, the mark of a hand with twisting, turning lines emerging from it could have indicated a journey's end; or it could be the artist's signature. I have heard you are clever at codes and thought maybe you could solve this mystery."

As the Indian finished speaking, the phone began to ring. When Nancy answered it, a man's deep voice said, "Is Mrs. Wabash still there? Yes? Tell her I have her stone tablets and papers and won't give 'em up. As for you, Miss Drew, don't try to help her. You're quick, but you're no match for Fleetfoot Joe. My spying on Mrs. Wabash has paid off. Now the Great Flying Bird is carrying me away." The man hung up.

Nancy stood lost in thought for a few moments, then returned to the living room. "Mrs. Wabash," she said, trying to keep her voice calm, "do you know a Fleetfoot Joe?"

"I've heard of him out in Nevada. He's only part Indian. A bad man. He steals things, then sells them to tourists as old artifacts he claims to have found himself."

Suddenly Nancy jumped from her chair, excused herself, and hurried to the telephone, repeating the words, " 'The Great Flying Bird.' Surely that's an airplane. But is it privately or commercially owned?"

She dialed the number of the River Heights Airport, got the information desk, and asked whether a plane had just left for New York.

"Yes," was the answer.

"Did anyone make a reservation for someplace in Nevada?"

Nancy waited while the assistant checked. The answer was no, and the woman could not recall from Nancy's description any passenger who resembled the suspected robber.

The young detective now asked, "Did a private plane take off?"

She was transferred to another office. There she learned that a privately owned plane had left ten minutes earlier. Its destination was St. Louis.

"The owner is named Robert Wapley," the speaker concluded.

"Thank you," said Nancy.

Before leaving the phone she called her friend Police Chief McGinnis and gave him a word-for-word account of what had happened since her previous report. He was astounded and said he would get in touch with security officers at the St. Louis airports, public and private.

Then he added, "Great work, Nancy! We'll have this Fleetfoot Joe in custody in no time!"

Once more Nancy returned to the living room. Everyone was standing, and Mrs. Wabash was saying good-by.

"Mrs. Wabash," said Nancy quickly, "what was your real purpose in coming to see me?"

"It's no use now," the Indian woman replied. "All the papers and most of the plaques I planned to show you are gone. I have no clues to offer."

"Clues to what?" Nancy asked.

Mrs. Wabash looked at the girl with tears in her eyes. "Clues to a lost treasure in the Forgotten City."

CHAPTER II

Safari Plans

EVERYONE in the Drew living room leaned forward in his chair, eagerly awaiting more of Mrs. Wabash's story.

"There are many, many pictures cut into the stolen tablets," she said, "but the main theme seems to tell when and where a treasure of gold was hidden. As you know, the ancient Indians in the United States did not use gold to any extent. Probably one reason was that it was too difficult to work with, and their tools were crude.

"It is a great mystery as to the exact nature of this treasure, but from what I can judge, the tablets depict several golden sheets. How big they are, one cannot tell. And when they were made and where they came from is also a mystery."

Just then someone pounded on the front door, and the bell rang loudly. Puzzled, Nancy went to open the door.

"Hi, Nancy! Surprise!" cried four voices to-gether.

Nancy beamed. Bess Marvin, George Fayne, and their dates were standing there, grinning.

"The surprise is great," Nancy replied. "Come in. I have a surprise of my own to show you."

George, a girl who enjoyed her boyish name, walked in first. She was slender and athletic look-ing and wore her hair short. Bess in contrast was blond with longer hair. She was slightly plump and pretty.

Burt Eddleton, George's date, was a stocky bru-net and one could surmise at a glance that he was a football player. Dave Evans, Bess's friend, had dark hair and eyes, and though he too was a foot-ball player, he had a much slighter build than Burt.

The young people walked into the living room and were introduced to Mrs. Wabash. "I am very glad to meet you," she replied. Smiling, she added, "I am Nancy's surprise."

Ned laughed. "Well, kids, the joke is on us. We thought we were going to keep a secret from Nancy Drew, and I find she's way ahead of us. She has a wonderful lead."

"What is it?" George asked eagerly.

Nancy requested Mrs. Wabash to repeat the part of her story she had already told, and then to continue with the rest of it.

"You probably wonder how I happened to

come to see Nancy Drew. A friend of mine who sometimes lectures at the University of Nevada, Professor Donald Maguire, has been trying to help me decipher the petroglyphs. The tablets came into my possession a few months ago. We concluded that the pictures indicate that several golden sheets were hidden, probably in the desert."

Dave spoke. "Mrs. Wabash, have you any idea how old the gold sheets are?"

The woman shook her head. "I am hoping that when they are found, they will contain symbols that will tell us their age and where the gold came from."

The whole story intrigued Nancy, who wanted to start out at once to hunt for the precious treasure. Each new case fascinated her from the time she first was asked to solve *The Secret of the Old Clock* through many adventures up to the most recent one, *Mystery of the Glowing Eye*.

Mrs. Wabash went on, "Don Maguire heard at the University of Nevada that Nancy was going on a dig out in the desert."

"I was what?" Nancy interrupted.

The other young people laughed and Ned said, "That was really the surprise we had for you. Some Emerson students and their friends are joining a group from the University of Nevada and going into the desert to search for a forgotten city, or at least some of the artifacts the ancient people may have left."

Nancy's eyes sparkled. "How wonderful!" she exclaimed. "You all did manage to keep the secret, and even though I accidentally came upon what may be a clue, you did surprise me. I think this is exciting. When do we leave?"

Ned replied, "We consulted your dad and he said you may go any time, but you will probably want to finish a little job he has given you. He thinks it will take two or three days."

Mrs. Wabash said, "Professor Don Maguire told me that Nancy is the finest amateur detective in the country, and that is the reason why I came all the way to River Heights to see her."

She informed Nancy's friends about the theft of her dictionary and her precious stone tablets and concluded by saying, "I don't know whether I have an enemy or the thief merely wanted to get hold of the tablets. With them he could try solving the mystery himself and find the gold.

"In any case, I have decided to leave this one tablet with you, Nancy. See what you can figure out, and if you can possibly trace the others, it will make me very happy."

"Thank you," said Nancy. "I'll make a drawing of this plaque and keep the original in a safe place. When I come out to Nevada, I'll return it to you."

Before saying good-by the Indian told the young people that a young woman in Nevada named Miss Antler might be of great help to them. "Try to locate her when you get out there."

Dave offered to drive Mrs. Wabash back to the motel and she accepted. Nancy's thoughts returned to the tablet, which she picked up to study.

Suddenly the young sleuth wondered if her eyes were deceiving her. A small figure in the lower left-hand corner was glowing. It looked like a scorpion, its head raised high.

"Look, everybody!" Nancy cried out.

As her friends crowded around the tablet, the figure faded. Though Nancy tried hard to explain what she had seen, the others thought the girl detective was joking.

"Nancy Drew, you're imagining things," Bess said. "I don't see a thing there. All those funny little pictures are on the other parts of this tablet."

No more was said, but Nancy wondered about the strange occurrence. The scorpion did not light up again, but through her magnifying glass, Nancy could see the arachnid plainly. She continued to study the scorpion. Had some trick of the sunlight coming into the room suddenly made it glint? She tried holding the tablet in the exact position she had held it before. Nothing happened.

"What is the thing you saw?" Bess asked.

Nancy shrugged and said she would get a book on wild animal life in the southwestern United States. Presently she came to the conclusion that what she had thought was an arachnid was a chuckwalla, a sixteen-inch lizard, which was harmless, although it looked menacing. She reported this to her friends.

"Here's something amazing about it," Nancy said. "The chuckwalla can wedge itself into a crevice and then inflate its body. This makes it almost impossible for an enemy to drag the creature out. By the way, it says here that at one time the chuckwalla was used as food by the Indians."

"Maybe," George said, "there was a group who called themselves the Chuckwalla Tribe."

Afterward, Nancy begged her friends to tell her more about the trip they had planned. Ned explained that it would be a caravan.

"There'll be trucks, cars, Land Rovers, and even a whole kitchen on a truck chassis."

George grinned and looked at Bess. "That's the place for you, cousin. You can cook all the goodies you want."

"Okay," Bess retorted. "I'll fix you. I'll make a tasty dish just for you and fill it with red peppers!"

The others laughed, and Burt remarked, "I guess that will hold you for a while, George."

At that moment the young people heard a car

turn into the driveway. Mr. Drew was arriving home. In a few minutes the tall, attractive lawyer entered the living room and greeted Nancy and her friends.

When he heard how Nancy had received advance information about the treasure hunt, he laughed. But his smile turned to a frown a little later, when he was told about Fleetfoot Joe and his attack on Mrs. Wabash.

"I'm sorry to hear this," he said. "Nancy, of course you've notified the police."

"Yes, Dad. They promised to call if there were any leads on the thief, but I haven't heard from them."

Ten minutes later Hannah Gruen came into the living room and announced dinner. Everyone went into the dining room, where the housekeeper had set a lovely table.

Nancy gave the motherly housekeeper a hug. "Now I know why you wouldn't let me in the kitchen," she said. "How attractively you've arranged the flowers! And what a delicious-looking salad!"

This was to be the first course. After everyone was seated, Mr. Drew said grace, then the meal started.

The group was about halfway through dinner when Togo began to bark frantically. He raced from the kitchen through the dining room and into the living room. Here he jumped onto a chair and gave a series of short, quick barks. Then he ran to the front door and barked again insistently. Nancy left her chair and followed him.

"What's the matter, Togo?" she asked. "Do you hear another dog outside, or is somebody at the door?"

The bell had not rung, but Nancy opened the door and let Togo out. Seeing no one, she was puzzled and ran after Togo.

Suddenly a man's voice cried out from the darkness, "Don't follow me! And call off your dog, or I'll shoot him!"

CHAPTER III

Vanished Guests

WHISTLING loudly and clearly, Nancy hoped Togo would hear her and come back. She called his name, clapped her hands, and whistled some more. The little terrier did not return.

Suddenly she heard a shot. Nancy's heart sank. Had the dreadful man carried out his threat?

"Oh, it just can't be true!" she told herself. Again she called loudly, "Togo! Togo! Where are you?"

By this time Nancy's friends and Mr. Drew had rushed outdoors. They could not see Nancy but could hear her, and set off in the direction from which the sounds came. Finally they reached her.

"What happened? What's up?" Ned asked.

Quickly Nancy explained and there were murmurs of anger and sympathy. Ned and George had brought flashlights, and now everyone searched for footprints. Apparently the fugitive had been standing in mud, and it was easy to follow the indentations left by his shoes. Right beside them were Togo's tiny prints. The group hurried on. Finally all the impressions ended at a main road.

Mr. Drew said, "The man must have entered a car here."

Bess's eyes were filled with tears. "Do you think he took Togo with him?"

The lawyer said he had no idea, but there was one thing of which he was sure: up to this point the dog had not been shot.

"Let's hope," said Bess, "that the man didn't take Togo away and kill him somewhere else."

It was a doleful group that walked back to the Drew home. Hannah had prepared a delicious apple-snow pudding with raspberry sauce. Everyone ate it, though there was little conversation.

When everybody had finished, Nancy said she wanted to examine the man's footprints. From a casual first glance at them, she was sure they would match those that had been left before by Fleetfoot.

Mr. Drew said, "After you do that, I think we'd better call the police, especially if the footprints do match those in our yard."

All the young people went outdoors, some to follow Nancy and the others to look at the prints at the rear of the Drew home.

"There are good impressions near the hedge,"

Nancy told the group, as she beamed her flashlight on the latest series. She was convinced they belonged to the same man, Fleetfoot Joe.

"I'll call headquarters," Nancy said, "and ask if there's any report on Fleetfoot."

When she reached the phone, Nancy changed her mind and called Chief McGinnis at home instead of headquarters. He was astounded at the latest bit of news and angry about the dog's disappearance and possible death.

"We have no leads yet on Fleetfoot," he told Nancy, "but my men are working on it. Up to now we assumed he had skipped town, but evidently he's still around. What do you think he wants?"

"I believe," Nancy replied, "he's looking for the one tablet he did not take from Mrs. Wabash's bag. We have it here."

During Nancy's telephone conversation, her friends scoured the neighborhood in all directions. It was possible that Togo had been shot just before the man got into the car and was trying to make his way home. After a twenty-minute search they returned to the house and reported failure.

Bess put an arm around Nancy. "This is dreadful, but don't give up hope. You know Togo is a very smart little dog. Let's hope that somehow he gets away from Fleetfoot."

Nancy smiled and gave Bess a hug. "Thanks. You're sweet to be so concerned."

The girl detective felt that with Fleetfoot still in the area, Mrs. Wabash might be in danger. She decided to alert the woman to the possibility. She dialed the motel where Mrs. Wabash was staying and was shocked at the reply she received from the operator there.

"Mrs. Wabash checked out and left no forwarding address."

Nancy was surprised that the Indian woman would leave without telling her, but perhaps she had received some message from home and had decided to go back at once. Nancy tried to learn from the desk clerk and the porter whether or not Mrs. Wabash had made a plane reservation.

"No, she didn't," was the reply.

She had scarcely put down the receiver, when Nancy heard aggressive barking at the front door. She literally leaped across the hall and flung the front door open. Her little terrier jumped into his mistress's arms.

"Oh, you're safe! You weren't shot after all!" she cried out, hugging her pet.

His response was to lick her cheeks, then jump out of her arms and race toward the kitchen.

Hannah greeted him with a joyful, "Togo! You're back! And you want something to eat. Well, I certainly think you deserve it."

Everyone had followed the little dog into the kitchen and George remarked, "If Togo could only talk!"

Suddenly Nancy leaned down and looked at the dog's collar. "Here's a note!" she told the others. Quickly she opened it, read the message, then reread it aloud:

Leave stone with pictures by old oak tree at entrance of abandoned mine in Ironton after sunset tomorrow.

"So Fleetfoot was here to get the plaque!" Nancy exclaimed.

Hannah beamed at Togo. "And this little fellow scared him away."

Nancy asked her father what he thought they should do about the note. He felt that it should not be ignored and suggested they contact Chief McGinnis. Once more Nancy dialed the officer's home and spoke to him.

Upon hearing the message, he chuckled. "You work fast on your mysteries, Nancy Drew," he commented. "Let me see, now. I guess the best thing would be to play along with this fellow. Suppose you find a stone about the same size as the tablet and wrap it up in a package. I'll send a plainclothesman for it tomorrow afternoon."

At once Nancy told him that Ned, Burt, and Dave were at the house. "Couldn't they leave the package?" she asked.

Once more the man chuckled. "Well you've made pretty good detectives of them, I admit," the chief said. "All right, you do it that way and let me know what happens."

After hanging up, Nancy had a sudden idea and she said to her friends, "If we give the thief a plain stone, he'll know right away we didn't carry out his wishes, and will probably return to do us more harm. Why don't we try to please him and yet frustrate him?"

George wanted to know how Nancy intended to do this.

The young detective smiled. "Evidently the series of tablets tell an important story, and perhaps even give directions to the treasure. One wrong link in the chain of pictures might spoil the whole thing."

Mr. Drew, who was in the background, listening, grinned. "An excellent idea, Nancy," he said. "What do you have in mind? Carving some petroglyphs?"

Nancy replied, "Exactly." She turned to the boys. "Tomorrow morning, would you mind hunting for a stone that looks like the one here?"

The boys agreed and took a good look at the tablet. Nancy found a short ruler and measured the length, width, and thickness of the stone.

Bess remarked, "This old tablet is quite reddish. Do you think you can find anything that color around here?"

Mr. Drew answered the question. "Over in the next county the earth and the stones are quite red. I suggest you go there."

In a short while the boys left with Bess and George to return to their homes for the night. Nancy and Ned stayed up for another hour while she made a careful drawing of the tablet that belonged to Mrs. Wabash. Then she began designing a new set of petroglyphs to put on the stone the boys would bring.

When the drawings were finished, Ned laughed. "That's misleading all right," he said. "You've turned a sheep into a goat, rain into sunshine, and a long line turning to the right directly to the left."

Both young people began to yawn. Nancy picked up all her work and headed for the stairs. "I'll finish this tomorrow."

Ned kissed her good night and said, "See you in the morning."

"Good night, Ned. Sweet dreams."

Soon after breakfast the following day, Ned set off to pick up Burt and Dave. In a short time George and Bess arrived at the Drew home.

Up in her room Nancy showed them the drawings she had made for the new tablet.

"It's so much like the other and yet so different," Bess remarked.

"The whole thing, I hope," said Nancy, "will

portray a misleading story to be put on the stone the boys will bring."

Bess looked at the work, then asked, "Would you mind explaining to me what all this means? It's worse than a jigsaw puzzle."

Nancy smiled. "Part of this is guesswork, of course, but here's my interpretation of the original story."

CHAPTER IV

The Wiretapper

BESS and George sat on the floor in Nancy's bedroom and waited for the young detective to tell her story. She held up the drawing and pointed.

"You see this big man here? I believe he was the leader of a group represented on this plaque. You'll notice he has something on his head that could be a fancy headdress. I understand that in ancient times the leader always covered his head to indicate this rank."

Bess interrupted to ask, "And this string of smaller people, who are they?"

Nancy's guess was that they might be his family or his servants.

George remarked that some of the human figures wore skirts. "Did women wear skirts thousands of years ago?"

"Apparently," Nancy replied. "I read some place that the skirt was really like a working outfit. It may have had pockets or loops through which cooking utensils could be slipped."

Bess began to giggle. "Imagine carrying a stone fork and spoon around with you for cooking!"

George added, "To stir up venison stew, flavored with some bitter tree roots. Probably better for you, Bess, than that sweet, gooey gravy you make out of chicken-leg gelatin and honey."

Nancy laughed, then said, "Venison is delicious if you have good strong teeth!"

She now continued with her guess about the meaning of the petroglyphs on Mrs. Wabash's tablet. "Whether it was the weather or the long trek or some other reason, I believe a great many members of the tribe became ill or died. This is indicated by the figures in the line who are lying on the ground.

"Then too some of them may have been attacked by wild beasts or poisonous scorpions or vicious birds. Here are pictures of all three. This is a bucking ram. Over there is a huge raven. And down here is a rock scorpion."

George asked, "Are there any poisonous scorpions?"

"According to this animal book, yes," Nancy replied. "They have slender tails and are yellow in color. It says here that the poison causes pain over one's entire body."

"Ugh!" said Bess. Then she asked, "How does a scorpion sting anyone?"

Again Nancy referred to the book and read, "The sting is located at the end of the tail. It consists of a very sharp, curved tip attached to a bulbous organ. This organ contains glands that secrete poison. It's like a poison reservoir."

Bess looked alarmed. "And we're going to find scorpions out at our campsite in Nevada?"

"Sure thing," George replied. "If you get bitten, it'll be a long walk for you back to town to a doctor. And of course the rest of us will be too busy to drive you there."

"You're horrid," said Bess, tossing her head. "Just the same, I don't want a scorpion to bite me!"

Nancy interrupted George's kidding to say that the article explained what could be done for a scorpion sting.

"First you tie a tourniquet near the puncture between the sting and the victim's heart. Then put an ice pack over the sting. Even better than that, fill a vessel with half ice and half water, and have the person completely submerge the stung area."

"Please, no more," Bess begged.

Nancy changed the subject and went on with her story about the tablet. "See this symbol that looks like a rake? Mrs. Wabash said it is supposed to indicate rain, probably heavy rain."

"I see it," said Bess. "Maybe these poor people were lost in a flood."

"That's possible," Nancy agreed. "At one time there must have been plenty of rain because this whole area was very lush and in places quite swampy."

George was skeptical of this. "How can they tell that?" she asked.

Nancy said mainly through the trees. "In the Valley of Fire in the desert outside of Las Vegas, there are pieces of petrified trees. They had to be submerged in water with chemicals in it for a long, long time before they became petrified.

"Also, by reading the rings on tree trunks, as you know, one can count the age of a tree because each ring represents a year. If the rings are wide that means there was plenty of water. If they're very narrow, there's been a drought.

"Apparently in the place where we're going to camp, the vegetation went from very green and watery, probably millions of years ago, to less and less rainfall. The result was that by ten thousand B.C., streams slowly began to dry up. Finally the area became a desert."

George asked, "What are these lines for?" She pointed. "They look like steps with no sides or support."

Nancy nodded. "I think it represents a stone stairway chiseled out of the rock by the people who lived at a certain spot. George, do you know what this means? The steps might even lead down to that buried golden treasure!"

George grinned. "Don't get carried away, Nancy."

Bess interrupted. "Here come the boys."

The three girls raced downstairs, and each asked, "Did you find anything?"

Burt took a slab of rock out of his pocket. It was a perfect specimen for Nancy to use for a substitute stone.

"That's great!" she exclaimed. "You boys are going to be wonderful at the dig in the Nevada desert."

"Hope you're right," Ned replied.

He took a package tied in cloth from a bag he was carrying.

"Here are some up-to-date chipping tools for you to use, Nancy. But, really, it isn't fair. You should chip as the ancient Indians did, with a sharp stone."

Nancy laughed. "I'm afraid I was born too late for that! Anyway, it would take too long, and we must hurry."

Before beginning her work, she studied the series of pictures she had drawn. Some of the figures were like the original but several had been changed. Among these were the stone steps. She had substituted pointed spikes joined by lines.

Nancy heard the phone ring. In a couple of minutes Hannah Gruen came to tell her that Mrs. Wabash was calling.

"Good!" the girl sleuth exclaimed as she left the room.

Mrs. Wabash said she had been threatened while staying at the motel and had been in touch with the police. They in turn had advised her to move out inconspicuously and to leave no forwarding address.

"I thought of returning home immediately," the Indian woman said, "but I wanted to see you again and talk over several things. I have taken a room in a private home. It's very secluded."

The thought rushed through Nancy's head that her own home might be bugged, and she had better find out.

Quickly she wrote on a pad, "Surround the house in case of a wiretapper."

She waved the note toward the group in the living room, and Ned came to her at once. He read the words quickly and gave orders to different friends to leave the house by the various exits. He would go out the front door.

The group hurried away in all directions, and in less than a minute the house had been surrounded. Ned spotted a teen-age boy hidden behind thick bushes in front of the Drews' brick home. He was holding a listening device against the house. Earphones were attached to the gadget.

"Come and get him!" Ned yelled to his friends.

Like lightning, he accosted the boy and took the instrument away from him. The youth glared at Ned.

"Just who do you think you are?" the eavesdropper asked.

"Never mind who I am. Who are you, and what are you doing here?"

The boy sneered. "I don't have to tell you anything. Let go of me. I've got my rights!"

By this time Bess and Dave had run around the corner of the house and had come up to the boy. He stared at them malignantly.

"Who is he?" Dave asked.

"He won't tell me," Ned replied, "but maybe he'll tell you."

"I'll tell nobody anything," the youth answered. "I got my rights. You have your nerve, grabbing hold of me."

Ned's eyes blazed at the insolent youth. "I want to know why you think you have the right to be here with a listening device. Who put you up to that?"

The boy refused to answer.

In the meantime Mrs. Wabash was saying to Nancy, "My name while I'm staying here is Mrs. Mary Morton, and I'm from New York City."

Nancy giggled. "Is Mrs. Morton coming over here?"

The Indian woman said she would not dare do so for fear of being seen and attacked again.

"Could you and Ned possibly come to my place this evening?"

"Of course."

As soon as Nancy finished her conversation with the Indian woman, she hurried out the front door.

When Ned saw her, he said, "Here's your wire-tapper."

Nancy looked at the boy, whom she had never seen before, and asked him who he was. The youth refused to answer this or any other questions.

"We'll take him down to police headquarters," Ned offered. "Unfortunately this wiretapping device is not a recorder, so we have no way of knowing how much of your conversation was heard."

Nancy heaved a great sigh. She was suddenly worried that the youth had heard about Mrs. Wabash's new name and the substitution of the stone tablet!

CHAPTER V

The Fake Tablet

As Nancy and her friends walked toward the front door, she said, "Instead of you boys taking this young man to the police, I'd rather hold him and ask the police to come here."

The others looked surprised, and the youth became angry. He shouted, "You can't keep me here! I got my rights!"

Ned spoke up. "You do not have the right to bug a person's home unless you have permission from the proper judiciary."

The boy broke away from the front door but Ned, who was next to him, grabbed the youth and yanked him back. Glaring, the boy said no more, and they all walked into the living room and sat down. Nancy's friends looked to her for an explanation of why she wanted to hold the suspect.

"We have no legal right to frisk this boy," she

replied, "but the police do. It's just possible he has a tape recorder hidden on him. If so, an officer can play it back. I'd like to hear what's been recorded."

She went to phone Chief McGinnis. Within a few minutes, he arrived with one of his men. They advised the prisoner of his rights and started to frisk him. He objected violently and began to fight. But he was soon subdued.

"Good guessing, Nancy," the chief said. "Here's a tape recorder in a pocket of his jacket."

The gadget was very small but efficient. The tape began with directions to Mozey from some man to spy on the Drew home. He was also to make a recording of any conversation he could pick up on the bugging device. Mozey had been told to bring it back to the boss.

"Who is the boss?" the chief asked him.

Silence.

The tape continued with conversations inside the Drews' house. Nancy held her breath for fear it would continue with Mrs. Wabash's conversation. But it ended soon after the telephone had rung and Nancy had answered the call. The young detective was relieved that it had not revealed the Indian woman's assumed name and temporary address.

Ned said to the chief, "Nancy quickly scribbled a note instructing us to surround the house and hunt for a wiretapper."

The two officers smiled. The chief patted Nancy on the back and said, "Good work again." He turned to the teen-age boy. "Come along, Mozey," he ordered.

The two officers left with their prisoner, taking the tape with them to use as evidence against him.

"I feel positively weak." Bess sighed. "What a day!"

Nancy smiled. "You can rest while I start chipping the stone the boys brought."

She went upstairs to get her ski goggles so that none of the fine pieces of stone would fly into her eyes. The other young people watched her work and were amazed at the precision.

First she took some hard white chalk and carefully drew the outlines of the petroglyphs on the new tablet. Since the pictures on the stone were very small, Nancy worked slowly and carefully. Presently she had finished a deer. A few minutes later she completed a shining sun instead of the rake symbol for rain.

"Anybody else want to try this?" she asked.

The only one who said yes was Dave. He was studying archaeology at Emerson College and could draw very well.

He exchanged seats with Nancy and picked up the tools. Dave used the tiny hammer and the little chisel meticulously, and a few minutes later displayed the figure of a sheep.

"They're perfect imitations," Ned observed. "Foxy Fleetfoot is sure going to be fooled."

Dave made one more figure, which looked like a cross. Then Nancy went back to work.

There was an interruption. A phone call came from Chief McGinnis. He said that Mozey's fingerprints had been found in their files.

"His home is in Gadsby, not far from River Heights. The police there said he had a record of petty thievery, car stealing, and participation in gang war.

"He's on parole, which, of course, he has broken," the officer added. "We'll hold him here. By the way, he still refuses to give the name of his boss."

"I have a suggestion," Nancy said. "Will you ask him if he was supposed to do an errand after sunset today for his boss." She held the phone for a full five minutes before the chief returned.

"I'm afraid my report is not much help," he said. "Mozey still refuses to tell the name of the man for whom he's been working. But when I asked him your question, he did look scared. I have a feeling he's afraid of the boss, whoever he is, and that if he says anything, he'll be punished by him."

Chief McGinnis promised to call Nancy if there were any new developments in the case.

"And good luck on your project tonight," he added, chuckling.

Nancy returned to chipping, which she finished hours later.

"Now comes the tricky part," she announced to her friends.

Bess giggled. "I'd say the whole thing is pretty tricky. What's this little thing down in the corner?"

"You remember the tiny lizard that I thought lighted up at one point?" Nancy answered.

"Oh, you think that's some kind of an identification mark?" Bess queried.

Nancy nodded. "That's why I didn't change it from the original. If it's on the other tablets, the 'boss' would notice at once that it was missing or changed."

"I see," said Bess. "Is the stone ready to be delivered now?"

"Oh no," Nancy replied. "Next comes the aging process."

Bess looked puzzled. "But you have to deliver it this evening. That doesn't leave much time for aging."

Nancy laughed. She called to Ned, who had just finished watching the final scene of an exciting western movie.

"Yes?" he said, reaching her side.

Nancy asked if he would mind doing an errand. "I'm not sure where you can find gypsum, but try the lumberyard first. I want a little bit of it."

Ned grinned. "I won't return until I have it."

The others asked what they could do to help.

Nancy's eyes twinkled. "Want a real dirty job?" she asked.

"No thanks," Bess replied promptly. "I have on one of my best suits, and I don't want to ruin it."

George gave her cousin a sidelong disapproving glance and said to Nancy, "How dirty is the job and what is it?"

Nancy told her she needed some lampblack. "Since we don't have any kerosene or oil lamps here, we'll have to use something else. I suggest black soot from inside the fireplace chimney."

Burt stepped forward. "That sounds more like a man's job," he said. "How much do you need?"

"Oh, three or four tablespoonfuls. Ask Hannah for an old dish and the scraper."

Burt went off to get the articles, then returned, took off his sweater, and rolled his shirtsleeves up to the shoulder.

At that moment Hannah Gruen appeared in the doorway with a large cover-all apron. "Put this on," she told the young man. Burt burst out laughing but obeyed.

At once George said, "Nancy, where's your camera? This picture is too good to miss."

"Up in my room," Nancy replied. George rushed off to get it.

Bess came forward. "Nancy, I don't want to be a quitter. Isn't there some clean job you can give me?"

"Yes. Take some of this chalk out to the kitchen and crush it to a fine powder with a rolling pin."

By the time the chalk and the lampblack were ready, Ned returned with some finely powdered gypsum. The young people trooped into the kitchen. Nancy was carrying the tablet with her. Now she spread a newspaper on the kitchen table and mixed the three powders together. When they were well blended, she added lukewarm water, about a quarter of a teaspoonful at a time.

George heaved a sigh. "Nancy, your patience is beyond me. Let's get this job over with."

Nancy smiled but said nothing. When she had what she thought was the right consistency of paste, she smeared it over the top of the tablet, temporarily obliterating the petroglyphs.

"This has to harden," she explained. "Then I'll turn the tablet over and do the other side. In the meantime, how about a little music? Bess, do you feel like playing the piano?"

"Sure."

The young people gathered in the living room. Nancy opened her guitar case and asked who would like to play. The others insisted that she and Dave take turns.

For the next half hour they sang old songs and new. Dave amused them with an original verse.

> "We're off, we're off
>   To the Forgotten City.
>   If we don't find the treasure,
>   It'll be a p-i-t-y!"

"I'll say it will be," George echoed.

Presently, Nancy left the group to return to the kitchen. She felt the paste on the tablet and decided it was hard enough to turn the rock over and "antique" the underside. This took only a few minutes. Soon she was back with the group, but kept one eye on her watch.

Exactly half an hour later, Nancy returned to the kitchen. This time the others followed and watched as she wiped off the paste. She saved it in case the stone needed another layer.

"I guess it's done," she said. "Now for the polishing job."

She put a little wax on a cloth, went over the stone carefully until it matched the original. None of the "aging process" rubbed off!

"That was a great job," Ned said to her.

The original and the new tablets were compared, and it was agreed that anyone except an expert on artifacts would be fooled by the substitution.

The boys could hardly wait for the sun to set.

As soon as it did, they left. Ned carried the new tablet, wrapped in brown paper. They rode part-way to the old mine, then walked the rest of the distance from the highway.

Ned was holding the package so it was promi-nently displayed. After a while he said, "I guess this is the right oak. Wow, it's a whopper!"

He laid the tablet on the ground beside it; then the boys started walking back to the main road.

In the meantime, Nancy, Bess, and George had followed in Nancy's convertible. When they reached the old road that led into the mine, Nancy started up the overgrown dirt path. She stopped the car, and they waited. There was a slight jog in the road, so the girls got out and walked ahead in order to see better.

"There's not a sound," Bess whispered.

Presently they spotted their friends coming from the old oak and starting along the road. Suddenly, and without any warning, a gang of boys, who apparently had been hiding behind trees, jumped the three Emerson boys and vi-ciously started to beat them up!

CHAPTER VI

The Dangerous Hole

THOUGH taken off guard, the three football players from Emerson fought well against the attacking gang. Ned heaved one of them to the ground in a football tackle. Burt held two of them and cracked their heads together. Dave got one young gangster around the waist and pitched him off in a somersault.

Bess was screaming, "Stop! Stop!"

The hoodlums paid no attention, and the girls could see that the ratio of ten fighters to three was overwhelming.

"I'm going in there to help!" George declared, and she started forward.

Both Bess and Nancy held her back.

George struggled to get away. "I want to try some judo on a couple of those fellows!"

"Don't!" Bess shrieked. "They'll—they'll make mincemeat of you!"

Nancy said quickly, "Let me try something else first. I have a police whistle with me. It may scare them!"

She pulled the whistle from her pocket and blew a shrill blast on it. The effect was instantaneous. The attacking gang, apparently thinking the police had arrived, scattered in all directions.

Ned, Burt, and Dave looked startled. The blast on the whistle had been so unexpected and authoritative, that they too had stopped fighting. The girls now hurried toward them.

"Who blew that whistle?" Burt asked.

The three girls burst into laughter, and Nancy admitted that she had. "It's the first time I ever tried to play policeman, but I must say it worked."

"Yes," Bess added. "I never saw people run away so fast in my life."

The three boys laughed, and Dave declared, "From now on I'm going to carry a police whistle in my pocket, too."

Nancy grinned. "This isn't an authentic police whistle," she said. "You can buy one like this in any toy store, but if you blow hard enough on it you can really make a loud noise."

"I'll say," Ned agreed.

Suddenly the stillness was broken by a shout from the woods. The young people were afraid that the gang, realizing they had been tricked, were coming back to fight again. Nancy and her friends stood silently for a few moments, but no one showed up.

"Who was that?" Bess asked.

There was another shout, and then a voice called out, "You won this time, but watch out. We're friends of the guy you put in jail. We'll get you yet!"

After that there was silence. The group remained where they were for nearly a minute.

Finally Ned said he wanted to see whether the package was still at the old oak tree.

"Yes it is," he called out. "Right where I laid it."

George spoke up. "So the gang was not really after the package. They followed us only to punish you boys for having their friend arrested."

The young people returned to the two cars. Nancy and Ned climbed into her convertible. Ned took the wheel and they set off for the Drew home. The rest of the group rode directly behind.

By this time, nightfall had come and the moon was shining brightly. Presently Nancy detected a moving shadow among the trees. She asked Ned to stop and signal the other car to halt.

"Look over there!" she said, pointing out the window.

A tall lanky boy was warily hiking in the direction of the old mine. The next second he disappeared.

Nancy and her friends got out of the cars and watched for a few minutes, but did not see the youth again. They could still see the old oak tree. No one was near it.

Finally Nancy spoke. "I believe something happened to that boy. He must have fallen and knocked himself out, or perhaps he slipped into an old mine hole."

Thoroughly alarmed, the young people went toward the spot where the boy had disappeared, holding their flashlights.

"Watch out for a trap!" Ned warned.

The searchers walked carefully, surveying every inch of the ground before they walked over it.

"Listen!" Nancy said suddenly. "I think I heard a cry for help."

Her friends stopped short and waited for another call. There was no doubt about it when another feeble plea came.

"Help! Help!"

The group swung their flashlights around but could see no one. Nancy walked forward.

"I'd say that cry came from down below. Let's look for a hole."

The group crept forward, and presently George said, "I see it!" She played her light on the spot.

A tangled mass of vines had apparently covered the opening. Now they were broken. Flashlights were beamed down into the hole. It was deep.

"Help! Get me out of here!" a frantic voice cried.

"We'll try," Nancy shouted.

She examined the hole and found a rickety wooden ladder on one side. The girl detective beamed her strong light straight down into the hole and could see the lanky young man lying on the ground.

"Climb up the ladder," Nancy told him. "I'll guide you with the light."

"I—I can't do it. My arm's broken. It's no use."

"Then I'll come down and help you," Nancy offered.

Ned stepped forward. "Don't you think I'd better go?"

Nancy shook her head. "That ladder looks mighty rickety and I'm a few pounds lighter than you."

"A good many!" he corrected. "All right, but be careful."

Nancy had no trouble descending the ladder until she came to the third rung from the bottom. Then, without warning, it splintered and threw her off balance. She landed in a heap beside the stricken boy.

From above Bess cried out, "Oh goodness! Nancy, are you hurt?"

"No. I'm all right," Nancy shouted, as she scrambled to her feet. Then she leaned over the boy. "Tell me what happened to you. Didn't you know about this place?"

"No, and I didn't see the hole in the dark," he replied. "But how am I going to get out of here?"

"Can you stand?" Nancy asked, wondering if the boy had any further injuries.

With her assistance he got up. "I guess I'm all right except for this arm." It hung limp at his side.

"I'm so sorry," Nancy said. She then asked him to try climbing the ladder by using one hand for support. "I'll help boost you," she offered.

With the old wooden ladder now groaning and cracking, she managed to help him until those above could grab his uninjured arm and the back of his coat and pull him to safety. Nancy scrambled up the few remaining steps.

Ned began to question the boy, who said his name was Jim Gorgo.

"We'll take you to a hospital," he offered. "Have you any choice about which one?"

"No," Jim replied. "But I guess the River Heights General would be the best."

He was helped into the rear seat. "You're regular folks," he commented. "And I'm mighty lucky you happened to come along."

Nancy spoke to him kindly. "Jim, you're a very good sport. I know that you're in pain, but please explain why you were in that particular spot in the woods."

The rickety ladder gave way.

The boy took so long to answer that she and Ned thought he was being evasive.

Finally he said, "I might as well tell you the truth. A man sent me for a package that was supposed to be left at the old oak tree. I thought I'd take a shortcut, but now I'm sorry I did."

Ned asked him, "Are you a member of the gang who tried to beat us up?"

"Oh no," Jim replied quickly. "I don't know anything about that. I came here on my own. The man who wanted the package said he'd pay me well for getting it. I wasn't supposed to tell anybody, but you folks have been so good to me, it's the least I can do."

Jim suggested that maybe one of the boys would like to go back and get the package and deliver it himself.

"I guess the man wouldn't care as long as he gets the package."

Nancy and Ned exchanged glances. She asked Jim, "What's the man's name?"

"I don't know."

"Oh come," said Ned, "you must. Otherwise, how would you know where to deliver the package?"

Again Jim took a long time before answering. Then he said, "Honest, I'm telling the truth. I don't know the man's real name. He told me to call him Fleetfoot."

Fleetfoot!

Nancy was so delighted she could hardly keep from showing it, but she calmly asked, "Maybe one of us could make the delivery. Where would we find this man?"

Jim answered, "You know where the Waterfall Motel is?"

"Yes," Nancy replied.

"Well, I don't think Fleetfoot's staying at the motel," Jim said, "but he told me to meet him in the garden there."

"That sounds easy," Ned said. "As soon as we leave you, we'll decide."

In a few minutes the group reached the hospital. Ned drove up at once to the emergency entrance and went for a nurse, who came outside with a wheelchair. Jim climbed into it. Again he thanked the young people for rescuing him; then the nurse opened the door and pushed the new patient inside.

At this moment the other two couples drove up. "That boy is lucky," Dave remarked. "If we hadn't happened to go out there, he might have died of starvation in that pit."

The thought sobered the others, and there was little conversation as Ned turned Nancy's car and they all went back to the site of the old oak tree. The package was still there. Dave got out of the other car and brought it to Nancy.

"Thanks," she said. "Now which of you boys is going to the Waterfall Motel to deliver this?"

Dave said, "Suppose I do the errand alone. Fleetfoot has never seen me and won't suspect my motives are anything but good."

The two cars stopped some distance from the motel. As Dave started off with the package, Nancy whispered to him, "Don't try to capture Fleetfoot. I want him to get the fake tablet!"

CHAPTER VII

Petroglyphs

DAVE walked slowly among the trees in the garden of the Waterfall Motel. It was large and well kept, with meandering walkways among various flower beds. Light filtered from motel windows and doors.

"It's just dark enough," the Emerson student thought, "so it will be easy for me not to be detected as a substitute messenger."

Clutching the package under one arm, he sauntered along, watching the various paths but keeping out of sight.

"I hope I'm not too late," he told himself. "If Fleetfoot expected Jim Gorgo some time ago, he may have left."

At this moment, Dave saw two men coming along a walk near where he was standing. One was about five feet ahead of the other. Dave wondered whether or not they were together.

"Probably the one behind is a bodyguard for the man in front," he told himself.

Dave decided not to announce himself but to wait for some sign from the men. To his disappointment there was none.

They walked on for some distance. Then they stopped abruptly, turned, and, taking the same positions, retraced their steps toward the spot where Dave was hiding. Now he was sure they had come for the stone tablet. Was one of them Fleetfoot?

When the man in the lead reached Dave, the boy called out, "Pardon me, sir, but are you waiting for a package?"

"Yes, I am. Have you got it?"

Instead of replying, Dave asked, "What's your name? I can't deliver it to the wrong person. It's too valuable."

The stranger became surly. "Never mind what my name is, but if yours is Jim Gorgo and you have the package, hand it over."

Before the men had arrived, Dave had laid the wrapped stone petroglyph on the ground with a special purpose in mind. As he leaned over to get it, he pulled a miniature camera from his pocket. It could take pictures in the dark, without a flashbulb.

The whole episode lasted about two seconds. A picture was snapped as the package was being handed over.

Apparently the two men were unaware of what had happened. One of them quickly grabbed the stone tablet, and the two hurried up the walk.

Dave did not follow. Instead, he set the little camera in motion to develop the picture. When it was ready, he tore the paper out and walked toward a light. He had photographed the faces of the two men, and they were clear enough to be identified. Excited, he returned to Nancy's house.

"How did you make out?" she asked.

Dave wore a big grin. He pulled the photograph from his pocket. "Here are the men who came after the package," he announced.

Nancy stared at the two faces, then said, "Neither of these men is Fleetfoot, but that was a great piece of detective work, Dave."

"What will you do with the photograph?" he asked.

Nancy said she would take it to police headquarters at once and find out if these men were among wanted persons. "Let's go!"

"It's my turn again," Dave spoke up. "They may want to see my camera."

Ned grinned and made no protest. Nancy and Dave set off for police headquarters. Chief McGinnis was not on duty, but the sergeant at the desk knew Nancy and the story about Fleetfoot.

He looked at the photograph, then sent for a book containing pictures of wanted persons.

After a long search he announced that they had no record of the two men.

"They must be Fleetfoot's pals," Nancy suggested.

The sergeant nodded. He offered to have duplicate pictures made for Dave and Nancy. He would keep the original.

While a rookie was developing the extra prints, the sergeant asked to see Dave's camera.

"We don't have one as fine as this in our department," he said. "Where did you get it?"

Dave said it had been a gift from his uncle, who had partially invented the camera. It was not on the market yet.

Presently the rookie returned with the pictures and handed them to Nancy and Dave. The sergeant said he would discuss the case with Chief McGinnis, and some men would be alerted to watch for the two suspects.

Nancy and Dave went back to the Drew home, but the group soon decided to separate and return to the girls' individual homes.

"Breakfast at eight," Nancy sang out, as the others were leaving.

The following morning a phone call came from Chief McGinnis. He reported to Nancy that his men had had no luck in tracing the two suspects who had taken the package the night before.

"I'm afraid," the officer said, "that Fleetfoot and his friends had too much of a head start. They probably left town right after the pickup."

As Nancy finished the conversation, the front doorbell rang. The postman was there with a special-delivery letter for Ned. Nancy signed for it, then took the letter to him.

"This is what I've been waiting for," he said. "Our tickets! I asked the travel agent to send them here."

Ned opened the envelope quickly and pulled out plane tickets for the whole group. He explained that they would fly from River Heights to Chicago, then to Las Vegas, Nevada.

"We'll stay there with one of the boys from the University. He's going on the dig with us."

"When do we leave?" Nancy asked.

"Tomorrow morning."

There was a loud squeal from Bess. "Why didn't somebody tell me? I must go right home and pack. I haven't even decided what to take."

Ned reminded her that all she had to put in her suitcase were her clothes. Everything else was to be ready for them in Las Vegas.

"I burn so easily," said Bess, "that I'd better take plenty of suntan lotion and a big hat."

George asked, "Nancy, are you going to carry the precious stone tablet with you or return it to Mrs. Wabash?"

"I'll call Mrs. Wabash—I mean Mrs. Mary Morton, and do as she wishes."

Nancy phoned the woman and asked her what she wanted done with the tablet. At once Mrs. Wabash requested that Nancy keep it.

"You have a lot of people with you, so there is less chance of it's being stolen from you than from me. I'll be traveling alone."

"Are you going back home soon?" Nancy queried.

"Yes."

The girl detective now asked if it would be possible for the Indian woman to come to the Drew home and decipher the symbols on the tablet. "Do you recall what was on the other tablets?"

"Vaguely," she said.

Mrs. Wabash agreed to disguise herself a bit and take a taxi to Nancy's home. When she arrived, Nancy brought out the tablet. Mrs. Wabash began to explain some of the symbols.

"This wavering line means a stream. Over here, near the deer, is a cloud."

Nancy asked, "These two men with crude spears—what do they mean?"

"I believe," Mrs. Wabash replied, "that it indicates a fight between the men. By the way, notice that their crude spears are launched from atlatls. These were heavy pieces of notched wood. By putting the foot of the spear into this, a man could launch his weapon much farther than he could with his hands."

There was silence for a few moments, then the Indian continued, "I think perhaps the two men who are fighting represent two tribes. They probably had had a war, but there is nothing here to indicate for certain who won the battle."

"Maybe that's on another tablet," Nancy suggested.

"Possibly," Mrs. Wabash agreed. "The tablets had no marks on them to indicate the order in which they were to be read. I was working on that just before they were stolen from me."

The conversation was interrupted by the telephone, and Nancy left to answer it.

Chief McGinnis was calling. "I have a little news for you," he said. "I don't know how useful it is, though. Two of my patrolmen spotted the men in Dave's picture. But they declared they had already delivered the package and were innocent of any wrongdoing. They would reveal nothing about Fleetfoot, nor would they identify the man to whom they had given the package as being the thief we're looking for.

"Of course, we had to let them go," McGinnis continued, "but they'll be kept under surveillance. If anything else comes in, I'll let you know."

Nancy thanked him, then went back to hear more of Mrs. Wabash's story. She confessed to having thought the chuckwalla lighted up but probably was wrong.

Bess had been studying one of the human figures. She giggled. "This creature doesn't seem to be wearing any clothes but has a very fancy headdress."

The Indian woman said she had translated this to mean that the two figures, which she thought were male and female, could indicate a battle between the chief and his leaders and the common people.

"I believe the common people won," Mrs. Wabash said, "because of the elaborate headdress, which no doubt was taken from the chief and put on the head of the rebel leader."

George remarked, "That's a fascinating theory. It will be fun to prove it someday."

As they all stared at the other figures, Nancy, who had been using her magnifying glass, suddenly exclaimed, "Look at this!"

CHAPTER VIII

Say It in Code

IN the lower right-hand corner of the plaque, Nancy had detected an almost obliterated oblong mark.

"It has very faint petroglyphs on it," she announced.

First Mrs. Wabash, then Nancy's friends, looked at it through the magnifying glass.

Finally Bess said, "What do you think the marks represent, Nancy? It doesn't look like much to me."

Nancy waited for Mrs. Wabash to answer but when she did not speak, the young detective said, "Could this carving depict one of the golden tablets?"

Ned remarked that if it were, this was an amazing deduction. Nancy, now thoroughly intrigued, went for an even stronger magnifying glass, which her father kept in a desk drawer. She trained it on the faint petroglyph.

"This looks like a man gathering something from a stream. I think this hairline mark indicates a stream. Maybe he has found gold nuggets and will make a plate from them!"

She handed the magnifying glass to the owner of the tablet. "What do you think, Mrs. Wabash?"

The Indian woman gazed at the symbol a long time. "I believe you're right, Nancy," she said, smiling.

She added that Nancy had made a valuable contribution to the mystery. "I would even guess that the long-forgotten city ran along the banks of this stream. The golden plates perhaps were made from nuggets found there, and the plates are hidden in that area."

Bess sighed. "Do you think we can ever find that city and the sheets of gold?"

"I'll wager," said Burt, "that if anybody can find them Nancy Drew can."

The young sleuth grinned. "It's a big order, but I hope you're right."

Mrs. Wabash rose to leave. She said she would meet the young people in Las Vegas.

"I'll memorize your address there, so if anybody takes my purse again, it won't reveal where you are."

Nancy thanked her for thinking of this. "Now

my friends and I will memorize your address and phone number."

They all repeated it several times, then said good-by to the Indian woman. Soon afterward the three couples separated to attend to their packing.

Early the next morning they gathered again at Nancy's house, and Mr. Drew said he would drive them all to the airport. Hannah Gruen bid them farewell, her eyes moist with affection. She pleaded with Nancy to be careful of Fleetfoot and of poisonous serpents or reptiles like the gila monster.

"I'll do my best to avoid them," Nancy agreed.

She hugged the housekeeper affectionately and hurried to the car.

On the way to the airport Nancy said to the others, "Don't you think it would be a good idea if we had a signaling system in code?"

"Great," Ned agreed. "You mean hand signals?"

"No, that is too obvious," Nancy replied. "How about three or four sentences? The third word in each sentence will be a message to the rest of us."

"Give us an example," Dave suggested.

The girl detective thought a few moments, then said, "I always suspect bargains. Sometimes I'm standing near a sales counter. I inspect nearby merchandise also."

For a couple of seconds her listeners looked

blank, but Mr. Drew said, "I get it. The message is, 'Suspect standing nearby.' "

"Pretty cool," Burt commented. "Anybody else smart enough to think of one?"

At first nobody answered, but finally George grinned and said:

> Please, Santa, look in my empty sock.
> Fill it up real high.
> A hole's in the toe, but never mind.
> The Christmas tree won't sigh.

The others burst into laughter. Dave thought it was a bit corny, but George's message was good. "It said, 'Look up in tree.' "

By this time, Mr. Drew had reached the airport, and farewells were exchanged. When the travelers arrived at O'Hare Airport in Chicago, they learned that the plane to Las Vegas would be late.

"We have a long wait," Bess complained. "I'm going for a tall chocolate float."

The three boys said they would rather take a walk. Nancy and George went with Bess to the concourse for a cool drink. On the way back to the gate at which they would board the plane, Nancy bought a newspaper.

She had soon scanned the first page and turned over to the next one. Suddenly she exclaimed, "Oh!"

"Bad news?" George asked.

"I don't know," Nancy replied. She pointed to a headline which read:

RUMOR OF GOLD IN NEVADA DESERT
RUSH TO SPOT EXPECTED

"Is it where we're going?" Bess asked. "And do they mean the gold——"

George grabbed her cousin's arm before she had a chance to give away their secret to anyone who might be snooping.

"Here's a map of the area," Nancy said, pointing it out in the paper.

The three girls studied it carefully and finally Nancy said, "Apparently it's in the opposite direction from the one we'll take out of Las Vegas."

Bess sighed with relief. "Thank goodness. We've had enough trouble with strangers already."

In a few minutes the boys rejoined the girls and Nancy showed them the newspaper story.

Ned whistled. "I hope none of the gold seekers come our way. That would spoil everything."

As the group walked toward the boarding area, Nancy said suddenly, "What number are we? It's like being in a maze. We'd better watch carefully for our sign."

For a couple of seconds her friends said nothing. To an outsider Nancy's conversation would seem perfectly rational. To her friends, using the third word in each sentence, she was saying, "Are being watch."

One by one, members of Nancy's group found an excuse to turn around completely to see who was watching them. All agreed upon a casually dressed young man. He seemed to be walking around aimlessly, but he always stayed close enough to hear as much of the young people's conversation as possible. When he realized that they had detected his purpose, the man hurried away.

"One thing I'm sure of," said Nancy, "is that he is not going on our plane. But he may want to make certain we're aboard so that he can telephone the news to someone in Las Vegas."

The trip to the Southwest was uneventful. On their arrival the young people taxied into the city in two cabs. They exclaimed over the garish downtown area.

"There must be billions of electric lights on these hotels, restaurants, and clubs," remarked Bess, who was riding with Nancy.

It was a busy city, with taxis and private cars going up and down the streets in a steady stream. In a little while their cabs reached the residential area, which was very attractive and much quieter. The cabs pulled up in front of Neil Anderson's home. It was spacious and had a beautiful flower garden.

Neil and his parents were charming people who made the visitors feel at home at once. A girl who was about fourteen years old came into the room and was introduced as Debbie, Neil's younger sister.

"I'll take you to your rooms," she offered.

On the way through the split-level house, they passed the dining room. In it was a very long table set up as if for a banquet.

Debbie saw the looks of surprise on the visitors' faces. "Big party here tonight," she explained. "The rest of the Emerson group is in town and all the people going on the dig are coming here to dinner."

"That's great," said Nancy. "Now we'll be able to meet everyone. Debbie, I just can't wait to see our caravan."

"It's pretty super," the girl said. "I wish I could go on the dig, but they tell me I'm not old enough. I guess because I have so many little accidents, they think I don't know how to be careful. I might ruin something precious that's dug up." She giggled.

"We'll take lots of pictures," Bess said kindly. "We'll see that you get some."

Since the dinner hour was only thirty minutes away, the young people quickly bathed and changed their clothes.

By the time they appeared, the other diggers

had arrived. There were introductions, a lot of conversation, and a great deal of laughter.

Nancy was thrilled. What fun it was to join this jolly group and to try solving the mystery of the Forgotten City!

After dinner, the young people gathered in the garden. A graduate student from the University of Nevada, named Archie Arnow, immediately walked over to Nancy's side to speak to her. At first she answered his questions lightly, but eventually she realized that he was trying to get information from her.

"I'll pretend not to notice this," she thought, giving him vague answers.

Several times Nancy tried moving away from him so she might talk to other people. He followed her very closely, and before she could say anything to her new friends, he would ask her another question.

"What a pest he is!" she told herself.

Nancy spotted Neil Anderson at one side of the garden. She made a sudden move, wedged her way through a group, and managed to get to Neil before Archie was aware of what had happened. Quickly Nancy asked Neil what kind of a person Archie was.

"Oh, he's an archaeological whiz," Neil replied, "but he's not well liked. He's very opinionated and secretive. Be careful, Nancy, or he may try to solve your mysteries for you."

Nancy smiled. "Thanks for the tip."

She said Archie had been following her around and asking questions. "I don't know how much he has heard about what we're going to hunt for out on the desert, so I thought it best not to tell him anything I knew."

"You were wise, Nancy," Neil said, "and you'd better warn your friends."

Nancy alerted each one in her group.

George made a wry face. "I didn't like Archie from the moment I met him. I wondered how you could be so patient, talking to him as long as you did."

Nancy chuckled. "I couldn't get away, but he didn't learn anything from me."

The following morning Nancy telephoned her home in River Heights. Hannah Gruen answered and told her that the police had phoned.

"They reported that Fleetfoot Joe had definitely left town," she said. "McGinnis had phoned the Las Vegas police to be on the alert. So far he has heard nothing and suggested that if you should call, I should tell you to phone the police out there for information."

Nancy did so at once but was told there was no news of the elusive thief.

As she left the phone, Nancy saw Ned coming toward her. She relayed her latest clue.

"Keep your eyes open," he urged her.

Ned now told Nancy that he and the other

boys would be busy the following day, helping to get the caravan ready.

"Is there anything we can do?" Nancy asked.

Ned shook his head. "Why don't you girls go off and do some sightseeing in town?"

"I'd rather go out in the desert and visit the Lost City Museum."

George and Bess were intrigued by this idea and immediately agreed to go with her. Nancy rented a car the next day and the three set off. The place was about fifty miles from Las Vegas and was situated in a desolate spot.

The museum was an attractive oblong tan stucco building. In front was a beautiful Palo-Verde tree, which was unusual because everything about it was green—bark, stems, and leaves.

The girls were welcomed by a friendly man who said he was the curator. He offered to show them through the museum and explained that everything in it had come from the surrounding area.

"Are you girls interested in archaeology?" he asked.

"Yes we are," Nancy replied. "In fact, we're part of the group of diggers who are coming out to the desert tomorrow to work for a little while."

The curator smiled and said he was glad to hear it. "Where are you going to locate?" he asked.

"Above the Forgotten City," Nancy answered.

"Which one?" the man queried. "You know the Indian villages were strung along the Muddy River for some thirty miles. Of course, now they're all buried. In fact, you wouldn't believe it but four civilizations are buried in this territory."

"Four?" Bess asked in astonishment.

"That's right," he said. "Their civilizations were built one on top of another. The top one was settled by people we here at the museum call the pit dwellers. This is because they built their dwellings or houses partially underground. Come outside and I'll show you some that have been restored."

He led the girls toward beehive-shaped clay huts. They were reddish tan in color. The visitors peered inside the first one. In the center of the floor were the remains of a fire.

"You see there's a hole in the roof," the curator explained. "The smoke went up through there."

"How do you get in?" Bess asked. "There's a doorway but no steps. Did the Indians jump down? I know from studies that they were rarely tall people."

"They managed somehow," the man replied. "But most of them entered through the roof. They climbed up a ladder to get there. Why don't you step down inside? I think you can make it."

Bess grabbed the sides of the doorway and put one foot down onto the floor. The next moment she skidded, turned her ankle, and went down in a heap.

"Oh, oh!" she cried out, pain creasing her face.

CHAPTER IX

The Weird Valley

INSTANTLY the curator jumped down through the opening and assisted Bess to her feet.

"I'm very sorry," he said. "I should have stepped in first and helped you."

By this time Nancy and George had come through the doorway.

"I see what happened," Nancy said. "Here's a little round stone. Bess, you must have skidded on it."

She knelt down to look at Bess's ankle, hoping it was not sprained.

"Let's see if you can stand on it," George suggested.

Bess found that she could but said it hurt to do so.

The curator spoke up. "My wife, daughter, and I live in the house connected to the museum.

My daughter has had nurse's training. Let's see what she can do to help you."

Bess put an arm around Nancy and George's shoulders and hobbled on one foot back into the museum, then out onto a porch. Here it was shady and cool in contrast to the heat outside.

The curator went to get his daughter, who was very pleasant. In a short time she had bandaged Bess's ankle tightly and the girl declared it felt much better.

"Bess, I suggest," the young woman said, "that you leave the bandage on until you can ask a doctor just what the trouble is. My personal opinion is that it's only a sprain." The others were relieved to hear this.

Nancy and George felt that Bess should remain on the porch while they looked through the museum.

"Okay," she agreed willingly.

The fascinating collection of relics in the museum included many different kinds of objects. There were arrowheads, stone spears, petrogylph tablets, bits of turquoise jewelry, pottery bowls, and scraps of baskets made from grasses.

"These baskets are probably the oldest things that have been found," the curator said. "The Basket Makers belonged to the first civilization that was here."

Nancy said, "Then some of the archaeologists have dug that deep?"

"It's hard to say," the man replied. "This basket might have been carried to this area in a stream, and picked up by someone from a later civilization. It's very fragile. That's why we have it behind glass."

The girls spent a lot of time looking at each article.

Finally the man called to them. "I want you to see something special over here."

They hurried to his side. He was standing beside a large case containing a complete human skeleton and many artifacts.

"This was a thirty-two-year-old woman," the curator stated.

George remarked that the position of the skeleton seemed like a strange one in which to bury a person.

"It was the custom," the man told her. "The Indians always buried their dead in the prenatal position."

He told the girls that the cause of the woman's death was a mystery. He looked at his visitors with a twinkle in his eye. "Perhaps you'd like to guess what it was?"

Nancy studied the objects in the case. Finally her eyes settled on a small stone plaque on which two sets of marks, one under the other, had been painted.

She said, "These lines are so jagged, they remind me of lightning. Is it possible that this woman was struck by lightninng and killed?"

"That's a reasonable guess," the man replied.

George, asked, "Do you have bad storms around here? I thought it rarely rained in the desert and that's why it's so hot and dry."

The curator said she was partly right. "However, we do have thunderstorms and when we do, they're dillies, let me tell you." He grinned. "When you're camping out in the desert, and one of those storms is coming up, you have to batten down good and stay under cover. The wind can be fierce, and sandy dirt and uprooted weeds blow all over the place."

George asked if this was what was called tumbleweed, and did it actually roll across the desert?

"Some of it, yes," was the answer.

The man excused himself, telling the girls to continue looking around. In a few minutes he returned with his wife. She was a smiling, motherly type of woman.

"We'd like to have you three girls stay to lunch," she said.

"Thank you," Nancy replied. "I'll accept for all of us."

She and George followed the woman out to the porch, where Bess and her "nurse" were sitting at a table. The others seated themselves. The curator said grace and Nancy was much impressed with his giving thanks for the works of the Deity, including the wonders of the desert.

Afterward he described the foods that might be found in the arid territory. "There are many uses for the cacti, even candy, and of course there are wild animals that can be shot and cooked."

Bess remarked, "You have such a pretty garden. Where do you get water for it and for yourselves?"

"From an artesian well."

Nancy was intrigued to hear this. So there was water deep under the surface. Maybe at some time this had been part of the Muddy River!

When there was a lull in the conversation, Nancy asked the curator if he knew Mrs. Wabash.

"Oh yes," he answered. "A very fine woman." He laughed and looked directly at Nancy. "She has a fantastic secret. Why don't you ask her about it sometime?"

Nancy and George were afraid Bess might say something, but this time she kept quiet.

"I'll do that," Nancy said, deciding to ask the woman how much the curator knew.

He inquired, "Where are you going from here?"

Nancy said the girls planned to visit the Valley of Fire.

"Yes, do that. It is a fantastic place—one of nature's great wonders. After you go to the Visitor's Center there, ride on ahead for a little way and see the Mouse's Tank."

Bess giggled. "What a funny name! What is the Mouse's Tank?"

The curator chuckled. "It was the hideout of a famous bandit."

"With this bad ankle, that leaves me out," Bess remarked.

"I'm afraid so," the curator's wife said, "You must climb to get there."

The girls learned that at one time the area had been very wild, but now there was a good road leading to it, and a picnic spot had been built below the Mouse's Tank.

When the group finished eating, the visitors thanked their host and hostess and their daughter, then drove off.

The three sightseers reached the first part of the Valley of Fire, where they looked around in awe, for they had never seen such an amazing sight. Enormous sandstone rocks were piled up, helter-skelter, to the height of a big hill.

Presently Bess cried out, "Look at that rock formation! It's the perfect image of an elephant!"

They drove on a short distance, then George asked Nancy to stop. "See that strange formation up there! I want to get a picture of it."

The rocks looked like three huge, perfectly formed birds' claws, attached to part of a foot.

"This is like a wild animal jungle turned to stone!" Bess exclaimed.

"It's too bad we don't have time to get out and walk among these rocks," Nancy commented.

George returned to the car and a few minutes

later asked Nancy to stop again. She pointed to a huge rocky mound surrounded by green ground cover.

"That rock looks just like a sleeping cow," she said. "You can almost imagine that it's going to get up soon and start grazing."

Nancy had been silent for some time. Bess asked what she was thinking.

The girl detective smiled. "I was just trying to figure out this place. Perhaps once upon a time the area was fertile and huge beasts roamed around.

"One could almost imagine that there was a sudden volcanic eruption that tossed out rocks and a type of sandstone lava. The great beasts and birds were taken unaware and had no chance to escape. They died from the gas coming from the volcano."

George looked at the girl detective. "Do you also believe the poor things turned to stone like a petrified tree?"

"Who knows?" Nancy countered. "The beasts might have been covered with lava that hardened. I suppose you'd have to crack the rocks open to see if there were any bones inside. Of course lava is so hot that it might have disintegrated the beasts' whole body but left an outer coating."

Bess sighed. "There are times, Nancy," she said, "when your theories are way beyond me.

I'm afraid this is one of them. Where do we go now?"

"To the Mouse's Tank."

The spot was deserted. The luncheonette-and-gift shop at the base of the rock was closed, and there were no cars around. Nancy parked and she and George got out.

"I'll stay here," Bess said. "My ankle doesn't hurt, but I'd better not do any climbing."

Nancy and George left her and walked forward. They were sorry no one was around to give them directions, but they finally found their way up to the entrance of the bandit's cave and walked in.

"This sure is spooky," George remarked. "What a place for a hunted man to hide! I wonder how deep the cave is."

Nancy reminded her that since they had not brought flashlights and it was late in the afternoon, they had better not walk very far inside.

The words were barely out of her mouth, when the girls heard a faint scream. Both of them tensed.

Had it been Bess who screamed? Had she been attacked, or was she trying to warn the girls about something or somebody?

CHAPTER X

Call for Miss Antler

"WE'D better run!" Nancy exclaimed.

She led the way toward the entrance of the Mouse's Tank, with George only one step behind her.

At the opening, they pulled up short. Almost in front of them stood a man.

"Fleetfoot!" Nancy cried out.

He looked up, startled. Both girls dived for him but the thief was agile. He turned quickly and hurried down the rocks to the road with little trouble.

Nancy and George scrambled after him as fast as they dared. Apparently he was used to climbing up to this cave and knew how to get down safely and quickly. Now Fleetfoot began to run and soon he far outdistanced the girls.

When they reached the ground, Nancy said, "Let's chase him in the car!"

She and George jumped in, and Nancy started the motor instantly. She swung the car around and sped off.

"Who is he?" Bess asked. Learning that he was Fleetfoot, she said, "Oh, be careful, Nancy. You know he's dangerous."

The man leaped along the road like a deer. When he realized that Nancy was catching up with him, he veered off and scrambled up the side of a huge rock.

"Let the old mountain goat go!" Bess cried out.

Reaching the top of the rock, Fleetfoot hurried down the other side and disappeared from view.

"Oh hypers!" George exclaimed, using one of her pet expressions. "Why did we have to lose him when we were so close?"

Nancy accepted the matter more philosophically. First she thanked Bess for warning George and her of Fleetfoot's approach.

"But I'm sorry we lost him just the same," Bess said.

Nancy went on, "We've proved two things, and both are important."

"Like what?" Bess asked.

"One is that Fleetfoot definitely is in this area. The other is that no doubt he's using the Mouse's Tank as a hideaway."

Bess nodded. "So now all we have to do is notify the police and they'll know where to hunt for him. Then we won't have any more to worry about."

George was sure it would not be so easy. "We can look for a lot more trouble from that thief," she predicted.

Bess added, "I suppose there's no use wishing, but I hope Fleetfoot doesn't find out where our camp is."

"I'll bet he knows already," George said. "He probably watches everything that's going on in this desert."

"And steals what he can," Bess added.

Nancy had not spoken for some minutes. She kept looking right and left across the uninhabited landscape. There was not a house or other building in sight.

Finally Bess said, "Nancy, you look concerned. Why?"

Nancy said she had been watching her falling gas gauge.

"It's almost on the empty mark," she said. "I hope that even when it's marked empty, there's a little gas left in the tank."

She drove for another ten minutes, then slowly the engine sputtered to a halt. The car rolled for another hundred feet under its own momentum and stopped.

"Oh, don't tell me!" Bess said. "It's a long way back to town—miles and miles. I couldn't possibly walk."

George said, "I don't relish a hike of twenty-five miles myself."

Nancy suggested that if they could get to the main road, there surely would be help.

"Bess, suppose you sit behind the wheel and steer. George and I will push the car."

They tried this, but after doing so for a mile, Nancy and George were exhausted. Bess pleaded with them to rest.

"You won't have to ask me twice," George replied with a groan.

She flopped down on the field at the side of the road and stretched out. Nancy, too, lay down. The two girls closed their eyes against the sunlight and soon were ready to fall asleep.

Suddenly Bess awakened them with a loud scream and cried out, "Nancy! There's a hairy scorpion on you!"

Nancy jumped up instantly, flinging off the creature. It crawled away.

"I guess it's safer in the car," George said. "Nancy, let's get back inside and rest in a safe place."

Another ten minutes went by. Then the girls heard the sound of a motor. Nancy and George got out. A car was coming up the road. They waved frantically and it stopped. A young man sat at the wheel.

"You having trouble?" he asked, leaning out of his window.

Bess cried out, "Nancy, there's a hairy scorpion on you!"

"We sure are," George responded. "We're out of gas. We don't have one drop."

The young man grinned. "I can siphon off enough to get you to the first gas station," he said. "I can't give you any more than that. I'm going deeper into the desert and don't dare run short."

Nancy thanked him for the help and said, "You're a life saver. Two of us tried pushing the car for a mile and that was enough. Our friend in the car has a sprained ankle."

"That's what I call hard luck," the young man said.

He had already hopped from his car and was now opening the trunk. In a few moments he took out a narrow piece of hose and measured the distance between Nancy's gas tank and his own. The hose did not quite reach, so he drove his car closer, then measured again.

"It's long enough now," he said. "Well, here goes." He grinned. "Open your tank and we'll get started with this life saving job."

Nancy unscrewed the cap and he did the same on his car. Then he inserted the hose into his gasoline tank and squeezed the air out of the hose with his fingers. He put the open end into Nancy's tank and the fluid began to flow.

He called to Bess to watch the gas gauge. When it reached a little above the empty mark, he removed the hose.

The young man refused to take any money, saying, "This is my good deed for the day." He wished the girls luck and drove off.

The rest of their journey was quick. Nancy stopped at a filling station, then went directly to the Anderson home.

The boys were there and Ned said, "The Andersons are taking us to a hotel to dinner. I'm sure you'll want to shower and change to something suitable. See you later."

The girls scooted off to their rooms. Twenty minutes later they reappeared, refreshed and ready for the dinner party.

The group was going to the hotel in several cars. Nancy and her friends set off first in the one she had rented. When they reached the lavish hostelry, the young people waited in the large lobby for the others to arrive.

"This place is ostentatiously furnished," George said. "I like things simpler."

"It's too noisy to suit me," Bess commented. "This town never goes to bed, I hear."

In a few minutes Nancy and her friends noticed that telephone operators were paging various guests and announcing telephone calls for them.

Bess giggled. "How would you like to have that name?" she asked, repeating the call for Miss Shirley Rainbow.

A few moments later there was a call for Mr.

Bill Verythin. The next few were simple names like Smith and Jones.

Presently the operator called out, "Miss Rosemary Bluebird! Call for Rosemary Bluebird!"

Nancy and her friends were laughing by this time.

"I'm sure," said Ned, "that these are names of people who are here incognito; perhaps famous persons like movie stars."

The others agreed and continued to listen eagerly for the next one. Suddenly Nancy, Bess, and George were electrified to hear a familiar name called out.

"Phone call for Miss Antler! Important call for Miss Antler. Will Miss Antler please answer the phone nearest her?"

The girls looked at one another and Nancy said, "Miss Antler? Antler? That was the name of the person Mrs. Wabash told us to try to find while we're here!"

Ned asked, "Do you suppose she has something to do with the desert secret?"

"I think so," Nancy replied. "Mrs. Wabash said she would be very helpful to us. Let's hunt for her!"

The hotel was large and there were so many telephones that it was hard to know where to start.

"This is going to be a real job," George commented.

Nancy suggested that the group separate and scatter to various places in the lobby.

"If you see a young woman at a phone, try to find out if she's Miss Antler."

The six young sleuths hurried away to begin their search.

CHAPTER XI

New Clues

MEN were making calls from most of the telephones in the lobby, but there were a few women. Bess and George had no luck with the women they approached. Burt and Dave, too, were unsuccessful.

Ned went up to a young woman who was evidently waiting for a long-distance call and was holding the receiver.

"Pardon me," said Ned, "but are you Miss Antler?"

The young woman began to laugh. "No—*dear.* I'm Miss *Lamb*kin. Ma-a! Ma-a! What can I do for you?"

Ned ignored the crude humor. "Do you happen to know Miss Antler?" he asked.

Again the young woman giggled. "Come now, is that her real name?"

Ned decided not to tell her. "Who knows?" he said, walking away. At that moment the young woman's call came through, and she began to talk with someone.

A little while later Ned joined the rest of the group, which had already gathered. Nancy had found Miss Antler, and now she introduced her to the others. She was a young Indian woman, very pretty and charming.

"I'm so glad you found me," she said in a musical voice. "Mrs. Wabash wrote to tell me that you were coming, but unfortunately she did not say when.

"I'm a graduate student of geology and surveying. This is how I became interested in the desert area. It was through some experimental work I've done here that I met Mrs. Wabash. Unfortunately, I left no forwarding address, so she couldn't get in touch with me again."

Nancy smiled. "That was a lucky telephone call. To be truthful, we have heard so many amusing names paged here, we decided all of them were probably people who were traveling incognito. We even wondered if you might be."

"No," the young Indian woman responded, her black eyes twinkling. "It's really my name but I am teased a good deal about it."

Ned spoke up. "Mrs. Wabash said you could help us in our search in the desert."

Miss Antler said she believed she could. "I was helping Mrs. Wabash translate the petroglyphs on those ancient tablets. Now we can finish the work."

"Didn't you know," Nancy asked, "that all but one tablet were stolen?"

"No. How dreadful!"

Nancy told her the whole story, including the few clues that she had.

"My friends and I hope the police will pick up Fleetfoot."

"I hope so, too," the young Indian woman said. "In the meantime, in my work I have collected stories and legends from the older Indians who live in this area. I think there are some good clues in them as to where some rewarding digging might take place."

"That sounds wonderful," Nancy told her.

"Terrific!" George exclaimed. "Could you draw us a map?"

Miss Antler smiled. "I was hoping that maybe you would invite me to go on the dig with you."

Nancy was excited by this idea. "Could you? We'd love to have you come."

"I'd love to accept," Miss Antler replied. "Since we'll be working closely, I want you to call me by my first name. It's Wanna."

"What a pretty name!" Bess remarked.

"I think so, too," Wanna said. "When are you going to start your trip?"

"We're planning to leave tomorrow morning," Nancy told her. "Could you be ready by that time?"

"Oh yes," Wanna said. "I'll bring some special tools and surveying instruments with me." She smiled broadly. "I'm really very excited about this. Will you be in touch with Mrs. Wabash?"

Nancy said she planned to telephone her that evening and hoped the woman would have returned from her trip.

"I know she'll be pleased that we found you," Nancy said. She gave Wanna the Anderson's home address; then the Indian student said good-by. "I'll see you all in the morning."

Bess saw the rest of their group arriving and soon they were all together. A big table had been reserved for them, and in a short time they were eating and watching an amusing stage show.

After they returned to the Anderson residence, Nancy called Mrs. Wabash.

"I've just come home," the woman said. "Before leaving River Heights I spoke with the police. They had heard nothing about the stolen tablets."

Nancy surprised the woman by telling her she had seen Fleetfoot at the Mouse's Tank and among the rocks in the Valley of Fire.

"We reported the incident to the Nevada Police, and they are hunting for Fleetfoot and the tablets he has."

"That's good," Mrs. Wabash said. "When do you leave for your trip to the desert?"

When she heard that it was early the following morning, Mrs. Wabash said, "Then I won't see you for some time. I'll be eager to know whether you find anything of interest."

Nancy told her about meeting Wanna Antler, and said the young Indian woman would go on the desert dig with her group.

"I'm glad," Mrs. Wabash said, then added, "Good night, Nancy. Have a restful sleep and a wonderfully successful dig."

After hanging up, Nancy had a hunch. Could Fleetfoot have hidden the tablets somewhere in the Valley of Fire?

"Or was he just about to secrete them at the Mouse's Tank when Bess screamed?" the young detective asked herself.

She determined that at the first opportunity she and her friends would go to investigate the place. Nancy thought about it long after getting into bed, but finally dropped off to sleep. In the morning she was awakened by George.

"Get up, sleepyhead," her friend said. "You'd better hurry, or the caravan will leave without you!"

The girls were downstairs in a little while. Mrs. Anderson had breakfast ready for the group, then they went outside to assemble. It had been decided that Nancy would keep the rented car, since she wanted to make some side trips in connection with her sleuthing.

By eight o'clock, the caravan was ready to leave. Despite all that the girls had heard, they were still amazed at the size of the vehicles assembled, and the equipment in them. One truck carried tents for the whole group. Another was literally a kitchen on wheels, with a smiling chef in charge. There was a large refrigerated car with so much food in it that Bess's eyes bulged.

George teased her. "Watch that waistline, cousin. But then, if you work hard enough, maybe you won't put on any more pounds."

Bess made a face but said nothing. She had a continuous battle with the problem of gaining weight. Furthermore, there was no advice that helped, and each time she began a diet, her friends teased her.

One truck carried all sorts of digging tools, shovels, and spades. On a rig in one vehicle was a drill with electric motors to run it.

Wanna had joined the group and now said to Nancy, "I don't think they'll be using that drill much. Archaeological and geological digging is mostly a matter of hand labor. I've brought some special sieves for our group. Also some drawing pads, pencils, and crayons. Everything has to be very precise and accurately reported."

Nancy took Wanna around to introduce her to Professor Donald Maguire, who was in charge of the dig, and to the students from Emerson College and the University of Nevada. Some of the latter knew her through her geological papers and lectures.

"Glad to have you aboard," said Archie. "I have a theory I want to discuss with you."

Ned winked at Nancy. If this should happen, Wanna had his sympathy!

The professor and the students, together with Wanna and the three girls from River Heights, climbed into various private cars and trucks. The journey into the desert had begun. Wanna was now seated in the car with the professor, leading the way to the spot where she thought they should make camp and work.

The trucks rattled along the road, then turned off and clattered over the parched sands far from the roadway. Nancy's group was intrigued by the beautiful, stately yucca plants with their clusters of white flowers.

"They're as tall as I am!" Bess said as their car passed a group of three plants in full bloom.

In a little while they came to a small rock formation from which cacti were growing. On one of them was a huge, beautiful pink flower.

"Oh I must get a picture of that," said Dave. "Ned, please stop a moment."

Dave jumped from the car and took two shots of the plants with his special camera. A few seconds after getting back into the car, the pic-

tures had been developed and he showed them
to the others.

"They're gorgeous," Nancy said. "You'll send
these to your uncle? I'd say his camera is perfec-
tion, day or night."

During the brief stop, a couple of other cars
got ahead of Ned. As a result, they were almost
the last to arrive at the site where apparently
Wanna had suggested they camp. They could
hear loud talking and angry shouts at the head
of the line.

"I wonder what's the matter?" Nancy said.
"Let's go find out!"

Bess was still being careful of her ankle and
said she would not join the others. The rest
hurried forward.

"What's up?" Ned asked one of the other
Emerson boys.

His classmate pointed ahead to a group of
angry, gesticulating men. "They can't speak
English, but they're saying that we can't camp
here!"

CHAPTER XII

A Deadly Necklace

IT was evident from the strangers' language that they were speaking Spanish, but it was so garbled that it was hard to understand.

Nancy and Ned walked closer to listen. The group of swarthy men were waving their arms wildly, indicating that the newcomers were to leave at once.

When no compromise seemed to be near, Nancy walked up to Professor Maguire. "I've traveled in Mexico a good bit," she said, "and picked up some of the dialects. Perhaps I can translate what these men are saying."

"Thank you," he said. "I'll be glad of any help. This is a bad situation."

Nancy spoke to the men in the vernacular of the Spanish-speaking province from which she thought they had come. At once they quieted down and listened.

"Perhaps I can translate what these men are saying,"
Nancy said.

The young detective asked them several questions, then turned to the professor. "They have heard about the gold rush and their directions led them here."

"Oh, is that it?" he said. "Well, tell them that it's many miles from here, probably a hundred in that direction." He pointed.

Nancy told the Mexican group that it was unfortunate they had come so far out of their way. She pointed in the direction they should take. "I hope you can get rides part of the way," she said.

The leader of the group had a long black mustache twisted at the ends. He wore a sombrero. The man looked at Nancy, puzzled. She knew what was going through his mind. How could a young girl living in the United States speak his language and also know where the gold rush was, since it was so far away?

She gave him a big smile. "I am so sorry you made this journey for nothing, and I wish you lots of luck in your search for gold."

"We will go," he said finally.

There were murmurs from his companions, but they obeyed their leader. The men picked up all their belongings and started the long trek across the desert.

Now work on setting up camp for the diggers, who hoped to locate the Forgotten City, began. A job had been assigned to each of them, and they worked with precision. Two hours later the place was ready for occupancy. Professor Maguire consulted his chart and called out the names of tent mates. There would be six in each shelter. Wanna was assigned to the tent where Nancy, Bess, and George would be, along with two lovely girls who were studying at the University of Nevada.

The tent in which Ned, Burt, and Dave were to sleep was not far away. The boys were with three other Emerson students.

By the time camp was set up, it was very warm outside and the group was glad to take shelter under the tents. When Nancy and George arrived at theirs, they waited for Bess, but she did not come. The Nevada girls were concerned.

"One can get a sunstroke out in this desert," said Betty Carr.

"I'll bet I can tell you where she is," George said.

"Where?"

"In the kitchen. It's already past mealtime and if there's one thing that bothers Bess it's going too long without lunch."

The Nevada girls laughed. Doris Dunham said, "I hope you're right about where she is but if you don't find her there, come and tell us. We'll help you hunt for her."

The kitchen was some distance away, but Nancy and George trudged there hopefully.

Actually both girls were worried about Bess. With her bad ankle, how could she have walked so far, even if she was starving?

Finally Nancy and George reached the kitchen and went in. There was a great deal of activity and a meal was almost ready. Bess was not there. Nancy asked the chef if he had seen her, but the answer was, "No."

Now George was sorry she had been facetious about her cousin. "The poor girl may have turned her ankle again and may be lying somewhere out there in the sand and dirt, literally burning up!"

Nancy said nothing. She had heard a car coming. Wondering if Bess could be aboard, she walked over to where it was parked. To her astonishment, and George's, the driver hopped out. Archie! He went around to the other side, opened the door, and assisted Bess to the ground.

"Where have you two been?" George asked at once.

Bess giggled. "Playing Cowboys and Indians. Only we weren't on horses. We were in Archie's car."

"That's right," the boy said. "We decided to see if those Mexicans really left and didn't plan to double back."

"And they hadn't?" Nancy asked.

Archie said pompously, "Well, with me following them, they didn't dare."

Nancy was disgusted. Bess thanked him for the ride, saying she had had a lot of fun. Then she joined the other girls, who assisted her back to their tent.

"I thought you couldn't stand Archie," George chided her cousin.

"Oh, he's harmless and he can be fun. But I must admit it was a bumpy ride across this desert. Those Mexicans were actually running. Can you imagine that in this heat?"

"No," Nancy and George answered together.

In a short time lunch was brought around to each tent. They were told that the evening meal would be served outdoors, and the whole group was to gather near the kitchen.

When they assembled at dinnertime, Nancy asked Wanna if she would tell some of the stories and legends she had heard from the older Indians.

"Glad to," she replied.

After dinner she began. "You know, until recently the Indians had no written language outside of their pictographs and petroglyphs. So a great many of the stories were handed down just through the telling of them.

"When the tribes went to war, mixed marriages usually occurred. The young people and their children adopted the customs of both tribes. So at times one finds a combination of cultures."

Nancy said, "Then the Basket Makers could

have joined other peoples, who wove more intricate patterns on their products." Wanna said this was true.

"What were baskets made of besides grass?" Ned asked.

"Yucca and apocynum fibers. Later the people made sandals to protect their feet from rocks, heat, and the thorny cacti."

Wanna paused for a drink of water, then asked, "Do you know the story of the Great Drought?"

"No," Bess replied. "Only the story of the Great Flood."

The Indian girl smiled. "That was only forty days and forty nights of rain. The drought here lasted for several years. The Indians who settled nearby were farmers who grew thousands of bushels of corn each year. However, one year's supply would have to feed a whole community for perhaps three years. Without rain and with streams drying up, there was no crop, year after year."

"You mean there was no fresh food for the people?" Bess asked.

"That's right. Besides the loss of corn for eating, piñon nuts and berries dried up or didn't develop. The wild animals, too, were affected and went to look for fertile lands."

"What happened to the people?" George queried.

"Some died, I'm sure," Wanna replied. "But

apparently most of them took their belongings and trudged off to find a new settlement along some stream." Wanna smiled. "Well, I guess you've heard enough legends about the ancient Indians."

"Oh, no!" Nancy exclaimed. "Please tell us some more."

"There's time for only one before siesta," the Indian girl said. "Thousands of years ago the people here declared that a white man had come down out of the sky, riding in a giant gourd. He was some kind of a god and promised to return again. So far he hasn't come, but——" Wanna grinned. "Maybe the modern airplane that travels here has taken the place of the flying gourd."

Ned chuckled. "The first flying machine!"

When Wanna concluded her story, everyone went to the tents to read or write. Nancy asked for another legend about the ancient Indians.

Wanna thought a moment, then said that turquoise beads seemed to have been part of the dress of Indians from the earliest times.

"I have a necklace that was given to me by a very old Indian woman."

Wanna opened her suitcase and pulled out a box, which contained an exquisite necklace made of turquoise and gold beads.

"I have had these beads carbon-dated," she said, "and they're probably five-thousand years old."

George whistled. "Five thousand years old!"

"That's right," Wanna continued. "This necklace was given to me by an old Indian woman whose son fell into a deep, dry well. When they finally learned about the accident and pulled him out, he had died of starvation. But while he was still alive, he apparently found the beads and put them into a pocket.

"The old woman had made the necklace herself from the beads and I argued with her for wanting to part with anything so precious. However, she insisted that I take the necklace and wear it and keep it with me always."

All this time Nancy had been thinking and finally said, "It's possible that the well was at a level where the first Indians lived; in other words, the earliest of the four civilizations."

"It's an excellent guess," Wanna replied, smiling.

A wild idea popped into Nancy's mind. "Why don't we find the well, enlarge it, and go down there ourselves?"

The young Indian woman shook her head. "I'm sorry, but now no one knows where it is. A freak storm filled it up, and all efforts to clear it out have failed, according to my elderly friend. Now it is totally overgrown with vines and weeds."

Wanna went on to say, "I've had some wild ideas about that well myself. I believe the water came from a stream with a vein of gold alongside it. But the well was abandoned years ago, perhaps because of the boy's accident."

The Indian girl said that while she could not show the girls the actual well, she did want them to see something else.

"I believe I know where an underground stream supplies a small spring that is above ground.

"I think the underground stream runs through a mountain, but at one time no mountain was there. Over the centuries sand and dirt have blown across the area and formed a high covering over the stream."

Nancy was eager to see the place. "Maybe we can find clues to the treasure in the Forgotten City!" she said.

All this time, Wanna had been dangling the necklace in her hand. Now she laid it down on top of her suitcase. George, who was seated near her, reached across and idly picked it up. She decided to try on the necklace and was about to clasp it around her neck, when Wanna snatched it away.

"I wasn't going to hurt it," George said.

"It's not that," Wanna said more-or-less in a stage whisper. "You don't understand. No white woman must ever wear this! She will become violently ill!"

CHAPTER XIII

Telltale Wallet

QUICKLY George laid the turquoise-and-gold-beaded necklace back onto Wanna's suitcase.

She said, however, "I'm not the least bit superstitious. I'm sure nothing would happen to me if I wore the necklace, but tell me, why do you think so?"

The young Indian woman looked steadfastly at the girl. "I'm not superstitious either and I hated to believe the story. But twice I've let friends of mine wear it with nearly disastrous results."

Nancy spoke up. "What happened to them?"

Wanna told the girls that one of the friends had been in a bad automobile accident while wearing the necklace.

"The other one developed some strange blood disease, which several doctors could not diagnose even though they were specialists."

"Did your friend die?" Bess asked.

Wanna shook her head. "Fortunately, no, but she almost did. Since that time I've had more respect for the warning given me by the old woman who gave me the necklace. She said no one but an Indian should wear it."

George remarked that this was like having a curse on the necklace. "Such beliefs belong to witchcraft and things like that. Sensible people don't believe in all those signs and omens Man thinks up."

At that moment Archie stuck his head into the tent. "What you-all doing?" he asked.

"Come in," Wanna invited. She told the young man the story about the necklace.

"But," said George, "I can't believe it."

Archie looked at her almost pathetically. "My dear girl," he said, "as you get older you will learn that there are many unexplainable things in this world.

"Much of it has to do with objects that for one reason or another should not be touched by certain humans. In this case it happens to be white people, and that reminds me of Egypt. Have you ever heard of all the white people who became ill after they had dug into King Tut's tomb?"

Bess said no. The others remained silent.

Archie went on, "It seemed as if the boy king's tomb was never to be opened. But archaeologists thought otherwise and went in there. They brought out all sorts of objects that had been laid with the body. After a while every one of those white men became ill.

"Doctors were puzzled and came to the conclusion that germs can linger underground for thousands of years. I agree with Wanna that none of us white people should touch this necklace."

His listeners said nothing. Archie Arnow, having decided he had made his point, marched off pompously. Now the girls burst into laughter.

"Okay, Professor Archie," said George, "what are you going to do when we dig down among the Indian relics here? Are you going to tell us not to touch them?"

Wanna now laughed too. "You win," she said, "but just to be safe, suppose I put this questionable necklace away where nobody can touch it." She hid the ancient jewelry in her suitcase, locked it, and kept the key.

The next morning Nancy took Ned aside. "Let's ask permission to visit the Valley of Fire. I can't wait to search for the missing tablets out there. I have a strong hunch they're hidden among the rocks."

Ned was eager to go and said he would locate Professor Maguire and ask his permission. It was quickly granted, and the couple started off in Nancy's rented car.

When they reached the fantastic conglomeration of red rocks, they drove as close as possible to one section, then started to climb. The couple followed a trail but stopped every few minutes to exclaim over rock formations. It became a game between the two to see who could find the most unusual shapes.

"Here's one that looks like a rock cactus," Ned remarked. "And sitting on top of it is a big bumblebee."

Nancy laughed. "You really have to use your imagination on that one."

A few minutes later, however, Ned grinned at one she pointed out.

"So you think that looks like a castle among the rocks with a moat around it." He chuckled. "If I stand up there alongside it, may I be the knight in shining armor?"

Nancy laughed and the two went on. They had carefully examined every crevice and hole to see if one of the valuable old tablets could have been hidden in it. They found none and went on, trudging up and down over the uneven paths.

After a while the couple sat down to rest. Ned leaned back and in doing so his hand came in contact with a paper. Turning, he gently pulled it out of a hole.

"It's a comic book!" he exclaimed. "Why would anyone stuff this in here?"

Nancy answered, "No one is supposed to litter this spot, so what better place than this to hide something?"

She had been smiling. Now she became serious, got up, and peered into the hole herself. Nancy had learned not to put her bare hands into such places in case there were poisonous insects or reptiles of any kind resting within. She beamed her flashlight inside but could see nothing alive. A small object was lying at the back of the hole, however.

"I see something," she said, reaching in. Nancy pulled out a somewhat dilapidated wallet. In it was a small amount of money and two diamond rings! As she replaced them, Nancy turned the wallet over. On it were two initials: F. J. "Fleetfoot Joe!" she exclaimed. "What a find!"

Ned said he was sure the rings had been stolen. Fleetfoot had hidden the wallet here until he thought it would be safe to bring it out and sell the jewels.

Nancy agreed. For a few seconds she sat, lost in thought. Finally she said, "If this is one of Fleetfoot's hiding places, maybe one or more of the tablets is buried around here."

The two began a careful search. They scraped away loose sandstone and cleaned out crevices and indentations.

Suddenly Nancy cried out, "I think I've found one!"

"Fleetfoot Joe's initials!" Nancy exclaimed.

The flat object, wrapped in a cellophane bag, had been wedged between two rocks and covered with sandstone scrapings.

Ned hurried to Nancy's side, and together they pulled the object from its cover. There was no question that this was another one of the tablets. Nancy took her magnifying glass from a pocket in her jeans and examined the plaque.

"Here is the identifying mark in the lower left-hand corner," she said. "The familiar chuckwalla symbol."

She handed Ned the magnifying glass. He was intrigued with the petroglyphs on the tablet but could not decipher them. He did, however, spot the same tiny oblong symbol in the lower right-hand corner that they had come to believe indicated the golden tablets.

As Nancy secreted the ancient plaque under her sweater and was about to hunt for another matching one, Ned suddenly said in a loud voice, "Run, because you should be in the shade. Desert sunburns are deadly. Any person being caught here is a target. Be on watch for sunstroke."

For an instant Nancy was puzzled, since she was not particularly hot and was wearing a big hat. Then, suddenly, as she repeated the words in her mind, she realized that this was a coded message to her.

It was saying, "You are being watch."

Without question she hurried along after him

until he stopped. He whispered, "A man suddenly appeared up above us. I'm sure he was Fleetfoot!"

Nancy was aghast. Now that he knew she had the tablet, the thief might attack both her and Ned! Then what?

"We mustn't let him harm us," she told Ned, fearing he might throw a large rock down on them. "And we ought to take this tablet back to camp as fast as we can."

There was a further whispered conversation. Ned felt that they should not return to the car the same way they had come.

"But we have to get back to it in order to escape," Nancy reminded him.

Ned thought he had the rocky area pretty well figured out. "I believe there's a shortcut we can take. It may be rough, but I think we'd better try it."

The two scrambled off the path, over a series of jagged rocks, and came to another trail. They hurried along this in what they thought was the right direction.

Finally Nancy said, "I have a strange feeling we're going in the wrong direction."

"Then let's turn around," Ned suggested.

The two hurried on. The trail ended. They looked far below them but could see no sign of the car. Furthermore, they could not see Fleetfoot or anyone else.

"Ned," said Nancy, "don't you think we'd better keep going down? Eventually we'll come to the desert floor, and then maybe we can figure out how to get to the car."

"All right," he agreed.

The couple went on, first down, then up, then down again. At last they sat down to rest. They could see nothing around them but jagged red rocks.

Not a word was said for several minutes, but finally Ned spoke. "Nancy, I'm afraid we're hopelessly lost."

CHAPTER XIV

Hidden River

AFTER Ned announced that he and Nancy were lost in the Valley of Fire, the two stood up and looked around. They were silent for several minutes. Each was trying to figure out which way would lead them out of this maze, and they began to walk.

Finally, Nancy said, "I wonder if Fleetfoot is still around. He seemed to be familiar with this place and probably wouldn't get lost."

"But if he tried to follow us to get back the stone tablet you're carrying," Ned said, frowning, "he may not care how far we go. In the end he'll outwit us."

The two walked on. Long shadows began to creep across the landscape. The stranded couple did not want to spend the night in the Valley of Fire.

Nancy had just rounded another corner between two huge rock formations when she cried out, "The car! I see it!"

Ned looked too. The car was almost directly below them but far, far down. Both he and Nancy wondered how much they would have to slip and slide down the steep incline to reach it.

The two held hands, dug their heels into the sandy rock, and slowly went down in a zigzag course. They knew this had been the way Indians ascended and descended steep slopes.

"You all right?" Ned asked, as Nancy's right foot suddenly skidded under her.

He kept her from falling and she declared that the slip had meant nothing. At last, to their relief, they were able to jump down the last few feet to the desert floor.

"Thank goodness!" Ned murmured.

They hurried forward to the car. Nancy wanted to look at the tablet again but thought it might not be wise. Fleetfoot could be spying on the couple, even with binoculars.

"Let's get back to camp as soon as possible," Nancy suggested as Ned took the wheel.

"If you don't mind the bumps I can go over this flat desert as fast as you want. What do you say? One-hundred or one-hundred and fifty miles an hour?"

Nancy laughed and this broke the tension. They stopped worrying about Fleetfoot and realized how lucky they had been to find the tablet.

"Only five more to go," Nancy said.

Ned groaned. "Only five?"

Barely three minutes had gone by when he and Nancy saw the bobbing lights of a car coming toward them.

"Oh I hope it's not that thief!" Nancy said, worried.

The other automobile began to blow its horn incessantly. Was this a signal for Nancy and Ned to stop?

"Don't stop!" Nancy begged.

Ned was debating whether or not he should shoot past the other car when his own headlights picked up the license plate of the oncoming automobile.

"It's one of the camp cars!" he said.

Nancy was sure it was a rescue party and knew the rescuers must be Bess, George, Burt, and Dave.

"Am I glad to see you're safe!" Bess exclaimed, as the vehicles pulled up side-by-side. "You had us worried sick!"

"Sorry," Nancy said. "We got lost!"

The three couples sat and talked from the windows of their cars.

"Did you have any luck?" George asked.

"I'll say," Ned replied. "Nancy found one of the missing plaques."

"Honestly?" George burst out. "Hypers! You're really getting ahead of that thief Fleet-foot, Nancy."

"But wait until you hear the rest of the story," Ned said. He quickly brought the other four up to date on what had happened in the Valley of Fire.

"Some adventure!" Burt remarked. "Well, we'll follow you back to camp."

The person most delighted over Nancy's find was Wanna. She looked at the tablet, trying to decide what the petroglyphs meant.

Presently she said excitedly, "I believe these pictures prove my theory that there is an underground river with gold nuggets on its shores."

Nancy said she could hardly wait to start a search for the stream.

Dinner that evening had been delayed because of the camp's worry over Nancy and Ned. But now everyone gathered for the outdoor get-together.

Each camper was given a large metal frying pan with wooden handles, and the delicious hot meal was put into this.

Afterward there was singing and guitar play-ing. Archie was in the front row, making wise-cracks and telling some corny jokes. Nancy's group had to admit, nevertheless, that the young man had a very good singing voice.

"He ought to stick to singing," Burt remarked, "and not try to tell jokes."

When the concert was over, Bess said to Nancy, "I'm terribly worried about your having the tablet. Suppose Fleetfoot or one of his buddies comes in here and takes it!"

Ned overheard her. He answered the question. "Don't worry. Several of the boys brought good watchdogs along. They'll take care of any prowlers." Bess felt better.

Her thought made Nancy decide to produce a faithful drawing of the petroglyphs on the plaque she had found. Then she asked George to walk with her to the kitchen unit.

"There's always someone on duty there, and I think they'll let me hide this tablet behind some of the food, where it won't be noticed."

The chef, who was just tidying up, was glad to have his place used for the hidden treasure. "Don't you worry about a thing, Nancy," he said. "I'll be like a watchdog around here."

It seemed to be no more than a few minutes between the time the girls said good night to one another and the time the alarm went off at five in the morning. Nancy, George, Wanna, and the two Nevada girls yawned but got out of bed. Bess merely turned over.

"Bess Marvin," said George, "you'll have to get up. We have work ahead of us."

Bess merely grunted. "Why do I have to get up so early?"

George told her that if she did not, she would be left alone all day. Did she want that? The thought made Bess climb out of bed instantly.

Professor Maguire, the students from the University of Nevada, and all the Emerson boys except Ned, Burt, and Dave, had already chosen a site at which to start digging. Wanna had received permission to take Nancy's group to another location. Bess and Dave borrowed a small sports model and would follow the others.

Nancy's car was crowded, with five people and all their working equipment. "I sure hope we don't get a flat tire!" Ned said.

Wanna directed the young man straight across the desert, which was only reasonably smooth for driving. The bumps set them all laughing, and made the journey seem shorter.

"We stop here," the young Indian student said a little later. "We'll walk down this hill to a water hole, which the Indians say is a spring bubbling up."

When they reached the spot, Wanna pointed out what appeared to be no more than a pool of water that came out of the mountain and ran back into it on the other side.

Wanna saw the looks of disappointment on the faces of her friends. "You expected more, I know," she said, smiling. "I believe that at one time this was a tributary of the Muddy River. By the way, now it's called the Moapa after the tribe of Indians that live nearby.

"I haven't quite figured out just what happened. Perhaps there was a great landslide, and the only spot where the water bubbled to the surface was right here. But that wouldn't have been enough for maybe a thousand people. So they moved out."

Nancy asked, "Do you think the Indians needed water badly and might have tried to tunnel into the river so it wouldn't stop running?"

"It's a fascinating idea, Nancy," Wanna replied. "Maybe someday we can find out. One thing I do know is that the well where the poor young man lost his life is very close."

"Let's not stand around talking any longer," Ned suggested. "Come on, fellows, we'll bring the tools down from the car and see if we can unearth this stream with the hidden gold plates."

As work started a few minutes later, Nancy reminded the others that they were not to dig fast and furiously.

"Remember," she said, "we are to take a shovelful at a time and put it through a sieve."

There was complete silence for a while. Bess sat down to work with a sieve, since her ankle ached a little, while Dave carried shovelfuls of earth for her to sift.

An hour went by. Each one in the group hoped

to find some ancient treasure, but so far nothing had turned up.

Nancy walked over to Bess and dropped to the ground beside her. "Would you rather go back to the car and rest?" she asked.

"No, no," Bess replied, "but what I think I will do is lie back and relax for a while."

Nancy stayed there and took up one shovelful after another of the soil. No interesting items showed up. She kept digging deeper. In a little while the young sleuth reached a very wet place. Was this part of an underground river?

She called to Wanna, who came over. The geologist was excited.

"Nancy, I think you've figured out the direction of the underground stream. Apparently it wasn't straight."

As she was speaking, Nancy dug up another shovelful of sandy dirt. She put it into the sieve and began to shake the contents.

"Oh, I've come across something!" she exclaimed.

Nancy picked up a small round object and cleaned it off as best she could in the muddy water.

"It's a turquoise bead!" she cried out. "Exactly like those in your necklace, Wanna!"

Before Wanna could pick up the gem, Bess screamed. "Nancy, throw that bead away! Throw it away! That's bad luck!"

CHAPTER XV

Gold!

AT Bess's frantic request, Nancy laid the turquoise bead on the ground. Now she looked
toward Wanna and asked her if she believed
the lovely little light-blue gem would harm her.

The young Indian geologist smiled. "No, I
think not. Keep it."

As Nancy slipped the turquoise into her
pocket, Bess set her lips primly. She said nothing
but Nancy knew she was worried.

"Please don't panic, Bess," she said. "At the
first sign of my becoming ill or acting strangely,
you take the turquoise away from me."

"I don't want it!" Bess said firmly.

The others laughed and finally Bess's dimpled
cheeks broke into a grin. "You win," she said.

The little group of young archaeologists continued to work industriously for some time before anything else was found.

George sighed. "This is becoming monotonous. If I could only find a piece of a bowl or an arrowhead or something, it would be more exciting."

Wanna looked at her. "Archaeologists must develop an unbelievable amount of patience. They sometimes work for weeks before making a discovery."

There was silence again for some time. Suddenly it was broken by Bess, who gave a loud squeal of delight. "Here's a real treasure!" she exclaimed.

Her shovel had brought up a small clay doll, which had broken into several pieces.

"You're lucky," Dave remarked. "If you like I'll help you put it together."

"Thanks a million," Bess told him.

The two carefully worked on the doll as if it were a jigsaw puzzle. Finally they figured out exactly how to put it together. Only one small piece was missing.

"Suppose you hunt for that little piece," said Dave, "while I go for the cement. It's up in the car."

While he scrambled up the hill, Bess took a sieve and carefully put the remaining dirt from the shovel into it. The missing piece was not there.

"Too bad," Wanna remarked. Then she smiled. "Maybe it will make the clay doll look more authentic."

Dave returned in a little while with a tube of statuary cement and half an hour later the ancient doll had been repaired.

Nancy had been looking on. Now she said, "Since the doll was not buried very deep, it probably belongs to the fourth, or top, layer of civilization here—the people who lived in pit houses."

Wanna nodded. "I'm sure you're right. Bess, you may have the honor of presenting it to the museum. The curator and the state will certainly be thrilled."

Bess would have liked to keep her interesting souvenir, but she knew this was against the rules. She must turn it in.

Meanwhile the other searchers had been concentrating on digging straight down, with the hope of eventually finding the underground river. By now the hole was fairly deep.

Nancy looked at her watch. "Time for a midmorning snack," she called out.

Everyone was glad to stop work in the terrific heat. At that moment Ned and Burt, suspended on ropes, were down in the hole, working.

"It's much cooler down here," Ned called up. "How about sending something down?"

"No," Nancy said. "Our instructions were to stop work at a certain time. We must eat and rest a while."

Reluctantly the two boys pulled themselves up.

Everyone sat down while Nancy passed around the food the chef had packed for them.

George served the cold drinks. As she walked around, she began chanting:

> Time to rest and eat
> In 102 degrees,
> Oh where is there a place
> Where I can slowly freeze?

The others laughed, and Burt suggested that the next archaeological dig she went on had better be at the North Pole.

All of them found that the ground was getting hotter, and they wondered how long they could stand it. While they were discussing this, the group suddenly became aware of a low roaring sound.

"What is that?" Bess asked quickly. It was evident she was nervous.

The sound grew louder. Then, before anyone had a chance to run, a geyser of water gushed from the hole where the boys had been digging! The force of the water soaked the young people and knocked some of them down. The others scattered.

The water continued to squirt from the hole. Everyone was wet but uninjured.

As suddenly as it had shot up, the stream subsided. Not another drop came from the big hole.

"Thank goodness Nancy made us come top-side," Ned remarked to Burt.

"Yes, we'd have shot into the air like a couple of rubber clowns," Burt replied.

"That geyser was the strangest thing I ever saw," George commented. "Wanna, what's the explanation for such a phenomenon?"

The geologist said there could be several explanations, but the one she favored was that the geyser had come from the underground river. Something had given it great impetus. The stream must have found an opening, and the force behind it had sent the water shooting into the air.

"Now that force is gone," she said. "It's my guess the river is continuing to run along peacefully."

Nancy wondered if such a geyser had ever erupted down at the water hole. Perhaps this was how it had been formed in the first place. Everyone in the group continued to talk for some time about the strange phenomenon.

Then George remarked, "You know I was singing about giving me a place to freeze. That geyser was like ice water, but it sure felt good."

In the heat not only their clothes but the terrain dried up in a very short time.

"I'd like to go down to the bottom of that hole and investigate," Ned said.

There was a short discussion about this. Some thought it was too dangerous. There might be a cave-in, or another geyser might shoot up.

Ned laughed. "Let's take a vote! Everybody in favor of my going, put up a hand!"

Bess and Dave did not raise theirs, but they were the only ones who were opposed. Ned was tied securely, and the other boys held the rope to help him descend slowly. George grabbed the end of it to lend extra strength if necessary.

Ned reported that while the sides of the hole were muddy and it grew narrower, he could see the bottom with his strong flashlight.

"It looks like water down there all right," he said.

For several minutes there was no report, and the two holding the rope began to wonder if everything was all right.

Finally Burt called down, "You okay?"

There was a muffled answer of "Yes, I'm okay. This is some hole."

Less than a minute later, there was a tug on the rope, and slowly Dave and George pulled Ned to the surface. He was a sight, and the others began to laugh. Ned was covered from head to foot with mud.

He ignored the laughter and said, "He who laughs last laughs best. This time I have the last laugh. Look here!"

Ned held up a gold nugget.

Now everyone became excited. Ned said he was sure that he had reached the underground river. "Digging along its banks may reveal an ancient Indian village—the Forgotten City."

Nancy's eyes were shining with excitement as she added, "And eventually the golden sheets!"

Wanna was happy too. But she was less demonstrative.

"We mustn't allow ourselves to be disappointed if we're wrong," she said, "even though I want to believe this fairy tale as much as you do."

Nancy advised that the group keep the whole matter a secret. "I'm afraid if the story leaks out, we'll be overrun with gold seekers!"

The others agreed.

Bess giggled. "Cross my heart!"

At this point the group became aware of a motor. They were surprised and looked up. Coming down the slope was a beach buggy.

"That must be Archie," said Ned. "He brought one of those along. Well, I'd better get down to that water hole and clean up a bit so he won't ask too many questions."

Ned scooted off, and a few minutes later Archie arrived. He stopped a short distance beyond the hole and jumped out.

"Well, I must congratulate you all," he said pompously. "This looks like a lot of work. How did you get so much done in a short time?"

George spoke up. "Oh, haven't you heard about the wizards of Emerson and River Heights?"

"Now what kind of an answer is that?" Archie demanded. "I'm part of this expedition. I have a right to know what's going on. Did you find anything?"

Bess dimpled and squinted her eyes at him. In a childish voice she asked, "Would little Archie like a baby doll to play with?"

The young man was furious. "I don't deserve such sarcasm," he said pettishly. "By the way, where's Ned?"

Burt answered. "Oh, he has gone to the Roman baths."

This remark was too much for Archie. "I'm leaving," he said.

In his anger he put his beach buggy into reverse gear and shot backward. The car backed into the hole!

CHAPTER XVI

A Skeleton Dance

FORTUNATELY the beach buggy was too wide to fall into the hole. The rear end had gone down but it hit the wall beyond, and the vehicle now hung over the rim.

After Archie's first look of fright and surprise, he shouted, "Get me out of here!"

"With pleasure," said George, walking up and offering him her hand.

He ignored it and got out of the vehicle himself, then surveyed the buggy bitterly.

Finally he said in a more conciliatory voice, "Come on, fellows. Give me a hand. See if we can push this thing over the edge."

Nancy suggested that they tie several ropes to the front bumper. "Some of us can pull, the others push."

"Okay," Archie agreed, then stood still, doing nothing.

The others tied the ropes, then Burt suggested that Archie go to the rear and push as hard as he could with him.

"Wanna and the girls can pull the buggy from the front."

This strategy worked, and in a few minutes the beach buggy was safe again.

Archie climbed in and started the motor. "It works!" he said. "Thanks a lot, kids. See you at camp."

The others were glad he was leaving but to be sure he would not be alone should his vehicle get stuck, Burt offered to go back with him.

Ned returned from his clean-up job. Since it was time to go back for the noonday lunch and siesta period, the diggers gathered up their tools and other paraphernalia. They lugged them up to the car.

When they reached camp, Wanna suggested that she and the girls go on to the museum and turn in the clay doll. Ned and Dave said they would see them later.

When the Indian geologist and the girls reached the Lost City Museum, the curator greeted them with a big smile. "I can tell from your outfits that you have been working. Any luck?"

Proudly, Bess opened a case in which she had been carrying the clay doll she had found and mended with Dave's help.

The man blinked. "You found this?" he asked.

"Yes, I did," Bess answered. "There were several pieces. We couldn't find the one that belonged in here." She pointed out the hole in one of the doll's arms.

"It was probably crushed underfoot," the curator stated. "But it hardly shows."

He accepted the doll with thanks, saying the state of Nevada would be very happy to receive this.

"Incidentally," he said, "you did a great job of mending this. Very professional looking. It is perfect."

Bess beamed happily, then she said, "We made a great discovery. I don't know whether Nancy wants to tell about it or not. We're trying to keep it a secret."

"Yes, we are," Nancy told him. She laughed. "But I think it's safe to tell you about it. We just don't want a lot of gold seekers coming to the place where we're working. One of the boys actually found a gold nugget way down underground."

"What!"

"That's right," Wanna spoke up. "As you know I have some pet theories concerning the desert. The students seem to be proving that my ideas are correct."

"That's wonderful!" the curator said. "Do you want to divulge any more?"

Nancy told him about the morning's adventures and the finding of the turquoise bead.

"But the greatest thing of all was the geyser." As the man's eyes opened wider and wider in astonishment, she went on to describe it.

"This is amazing," he said. "Why, you know, we might even be able to make this valley fertile again!"

At the remark George grinned. "And bring back American elephants and camels and even giant sloths."

"Oh stop!" Bess begged.

The others laughed and Wanna said, "All joking aside, if we could have a river running through this desert, it wouldn't take long before it became a good place to live."

She and the girls said good-by to the curator and drove back to camp. The cool quarters and hearty lunch were a welcome change for Nancy and her friends.

Afterward the other group of diggers displayed some of their finds. They had uncovered many arrowheads, some stone mallets, and a cylindrical stone about two inches thick and highly polished.

Professor Maguire said, "I believe this was a rolling pin, which the squaws used to crush corn into flour."

"What a weapon to use on an enemy!" George remarked.

Nancy picked up the stone. "Um, heavy," she

said, putting it down quickly. Then she tried rolling it. "In ancient times it seems to me people always did things the hard way."

"They had to use what was at hand," the professor told her.

At four o'clock that afternoon Nancy and her friends were ready to start out again. They could hardly wait to continue their work. Everyone hoped there would be no more visitors. Archie, meanwhile, had told the whole camp about the opening where Nancy's group was digging.

It was decided that the first thing she and her friends would do would be to enlarge the hole near the lower end. The diggers would take turns going down on the ropes, two at a time. For a while they turned up only pieces of broken pottery and stone axes.

"This must have been a large populated area at one time," Ned remarked to Nancy, who was his partner.

The young sleuth did not reply, for at that moment a trowel she was using hit something solid. Hoping it was a valuable piece and not just a rock, Nancy carefully worked around it. She turned her flashlight full upon the spot.

Then she exclaimed, "Ned, this is a bone of some sort!"

"Are you sure?" he asked as he moved himself to a position alongside her. The two worked in silence and as quickly as they dared. In a little while an elbow began to protrude from the sand, soil, and rock formation.

Ned whistled. "A human bone! What a find!"

Nancy's heart was thumping. She had never been more excited in her life.

"I wonder how much of this skeleton is here and how we're ever going to get it out."

Ned admitted that they would need help. Apparently the skeleton, if it was all there, lay beside the hole.

Up to now, the small amount of dirt they had dug had fallen down into the stream below and had been partially carried away by the water. For further digging they probably would have to remove a good bit of earth. Should it be dropped down?

Nancy suggested that they try to trace any bones they could locate without digging. This worked for a few minutes.

Nancy uncovered a hand, which had fallen from the wrist. Ned got up as far as the skeleton's shoulder and found that at the joint it was loose from the upper arm.

"I guess there are several pieces," Ned remarked. "We'd better get buckets and more help."

Nancy agreed. She and Ned pulled themselves to the surface and told the others what they had found.

"We'd like to see if we can find the whole skeleton," she added.

Bess said she could not believe such a fantastic find. "It's utterly magnificent!" she exclaimed.

Ned said he would suggest that they take an extra rope down, to which the buckets could be tied. The dirt he and Nancy took out from around the bones would be put into the buckets rather than dropped below. The buckets could be hauled up and the earth dumped.

Burt said, "You don't know how deep into the side of the mountain you may have to go. Why don't we take turns digging?"

"That's a good idea," Nancy agreed. "It's hard hanging in that rope sling and reaching in to dig out the dirt around the skeleton. The earth is packed solid."

Wanna offered to be one of the first to go down. She was eager to see how far above the water the skeleton lay. This might tell her which civilization it might have belonged to. She and Burt were the next two down.

The others took the buckets of dirt as they came up, and carefully spread the contents on the ground. While waiting for each bucket, they carefully examined the sandy soil for more relics.

None were found, but Burt called out that he was coming topside and bringing part of the skeleton with him. He appeared with an arm, though it was in three pieces.

The next time Dave went down and Wanna came up. George took a turn. They had found the left leg, which was also in pieces.

The work continued for a couple of hours until finally a complete skeleton had been unearthed. It proved to be that of a man. Wanna said she believed he was young and she judged from an indentation in the skull that he had been killed by a spear.

"Ugh!" said Bess, who secretly was glad that her ankle would not permit her to go down into the hole.

She liked the artifacts, but abhorred the idea of finding the skeleton of someone who had lived long, long ago.

"Let's wire this man together," Burt suggested. "I'd like to take him back to camp in one piece. Later the curator can do a better job."

Dave scooted up to the car to find the proper drilling tools and the wire. When he returned, everyone in the group became busy putting the prehistoric skeleton together. When it was complete, Burt held it up.

"He was very short," Bess remarked.

Wanna said, "Most of the Indians in this area were short."

Burt began to jiggle the skeleton and make him dance. The others laughed.

Dave said, "I have an idea. Tonight the whole

camp is to have a meeting around a campfire. How about our putting on a spook show?"

He outlined his plan.

"We'll all stay in the background. Then just as the meeting finishes, we'll make queer sounds. Burt, wrapped in a blanket, will come in, holding the skeleton and making it dance."

When Burt agreed, Dave whispered something to him and the other boy nodded and smiled.

Later, at the right moment, Nancy's group made low, moaning, crying sounds. Everyone around the fire looked startled. Then Burt stepped forward, intoning weirdly. He made the skeleton dance, then said in a deep voice: "I am from another civilization. Do not disturb my sleep!"

The whole audience burst into laughter.

At that moment Nancy suddenly felt a strong arm around her waist and a big hand was clapped over her mouth. Before she could resist, the girl detective felt herself being dragged away!

CHAPTER XVII

A Capture

FLAILING her arms and struggling to free herself, Nancy tried hard to loosen the grip of her abductor. Presently she realized that he was powerful and she could not fight him physically. She would have to outwit him.

"I must do something and do it quick!" she decided.

An idea that had worked before came to Nancy. In a few seconds she went absolutely limp, as if she had fainted. In surprise her captor nearly dropped the young sleuth and relaxed his hold on her.

The ruse had worked! Instantly Nancy was free, and she started to run back toward the rest of her group.

"Help! Help!" she yelled.

Her captor, realizing he had been outwitted, began to run. Several of the boys raced after him.

One lanky youth from Emerson College, who was a star track man, soon caught up with the fleeing abductor. He brought him down with a resounding thud.

Within seconds the other boys reached them and pulled the suspect back to camp. Nancy and her friends crowded around.

"Fleetfoot!" cried Nancy.

The man looked at her with hatred in his eyes, but he would not give up so easily.

"You can't hold me!" he roared. "I haven't done anything!"

Nancy gazed at him scornfully. "What do you call abduction? It's a federal offense. I think we had better call the police."

Fleetfoot now took another tack. With a forced smile, he said, "I wasn't going to harm you, miss. I just wanted to tell you to stay out of my territory."

Nancy did not comment. Instead she asked, "Where are the rest of Mrs. Wabash's stone tablets?"

There was no answer.

"Okay," Nancy said. "If you won't talk, we'll take you to the police. There's a warrant out for your arrest back in River Heights, and the Las Vegas police have been alerted to find you."

Fleetfoot looked surprised. He knew he was cornered and said, "Why don't we strike up a little bargain? If you promise not to have me arrested, I'll tell you where the rest of the tablets are."

Nancy told him she had no control over what the police might do, even if she didn't turn him in. "So it's no use trying to evade the law," she added.

Again Fleetfoot seemed to be thinking about what to say next. To everyone's surprise he blurted out, "Mrs. Wabash has the tablets!"

Suddenly a voice behind them in the darkness called out, "That is not true!"

A young Indian woman stepped forward. Wanna Antler!

She turned toward Nancy and said, "A little while ago I went to the kitchen and used the shortwave telephone to call Mrs. Wabash. She said one tablet had been brought to her by a man who was not Fleetfoot and had offered to sell it.

"The price was pretty high, but she decided to buy it. Mrs. Wabash recognized the tablet."

Bess exclaimed, "She bought something that actually belonged to her?"

Professor Maguire now stepped forward. "I think the sooner the police have this man in custody the safer we all will be. I'll call them at once."

Nancy whispered to him, "Fleetfoot is a slick person. Don't you think we should tie him up and put a guard over him until the police get here?"

The professor smiled. "I think it would be a very good idea."

While the boys tied up Fleetfoot, Wanna took Nancy's arm and they walked off together.

"I have a surprise for you," the Indian girl said. "The tablet Mrs. Wabash bought was the copy you made!"

Nancy was amazed. "Evidently Fleetfoot and his buddies didn't recognize it as a forgery," she said, smiling. "Otherwise I'm sure Fleetfoot would have blurted out the truth."

"What about the rest of the tablets?" Nancy asked.

Wanna replied, "Mrs. Wabash said that the caller had promised to return and bring them if she would pay the high price he wanted. Knowing their value, she agreed, but so far the man hasn't returned."

"It's my hunch," Nancy said, "that this man is a buddy of Fleetfoot's, and Fleetfoot isn't giving them up that easily. I'm sure if he gives them up at all, it will be only after he has had copies or drawings made. He'll sell them to Mrs. Wabash one by one."

Wanna nodded in agreement. By this time she and Nancy had reached their tent and were soon ready for bed.

Nancy was very happy at the turn of events. Not only had she uncovered something valuable for the dig, but she had helped to capture a wanted thief and was one step closer to solving the mystery of the valuable stone tablets, the golden plates, and the location of the Forgotten City.

She consulted Wanna, Bess, and George, asking if they didn't think it would be wise to go back to the Mouse's Tank and the Valley of Fire to make a more thorough search for the missing tablets.

"I do!" George called out.

"Yes," Bess echoed, yawning.

"Count me in," Wanna added.

The following morning Nancy asked Professor Maguire to go along with her group. He consented eagerly.

They started off in two cars. The professor rode with Wanna, Nancy, and Ned.

He said, "Suppose you call me Don. All year long I'm addressed as professor and it would be a relief to hear my own name."

"All right, Don," the others said.

When they approached the Valley of Fire area, Nancy said, "Let's start at the Mouse's Tank. We can separate and look inside and outside for anything Fleetfoot may have buried."

They reached the place so early that there were no tourists at the site. They examined the ground for recent digging and flashed their lights over every inch of the cave, but found nothing suspicious.

"I guess," said Nancy, "that if Fleetfoot had anything hidden here, he took it away after he saw Bess, George, and me."

They joined those in the other car, and together the eight went to investigate possible hiding places for the tablets in the Valley of Fire.

Nancy grinned and said to the other half of her party, "We've lost our professor temporarily. Meet Don, everybody."

They all laughed, and to make the change of name official, Bess, George, Burt, and Dave shook hands with Don.

Bess spoke up. "I'm glad you asked us to call you Don," she said. "I feel much more comfortable now. Professors always scare me!"

The others laughed, then Don said, "Where does the lady sleuth want us to start?"

Nancy suggested that they search in pairs. She handed out a whistle to each couple. "Every ten minutes I suggest we blow the whistles to be sure everyone is all right.

"Ned and I will be first to whistle, then George and Burt should answer, next Bess and Dave, and finally Wanna and Don."

They started up one of the trails, each searcher looking carefully in every crevice and depression for the missing tablets. Nothing was found, and in a few minutes the group separated, each pair taking a different route.

Nancy's imagination conjured up all sorts of ossified prehistoric animals. She pointed them out to Ned, who was amused.

"Yes," he said at one point, "if I concentrate real hard I can figure that the formation ahead was once a white polar bear turned red."

Nancy knew she was being teased and continued her search for the stolen tablets. Suddenly it occurred to her to glance at her wristwatch. Fifteen minutes had gone by.

"It's time for us to signal," she told Ned. "Would you like to blast a real long sound on the whistle?"

He put the whistle to his lips, and the shrill sound it emitted made Nancy put her hands over her ears.

A few seconds later they heard a blast from another whistle. Several seconds later there was a third. The couple listened for the fourth whistle. They heard nothing.

"That's strange," Nancy remarked. "Maybe Wanna and Don didn't understand. Let's try again."

The signal was repeated, but only two more whistles were blown. Nancy's forehead puckered. "I hope this doesn't mean Wanna and Don ran into trouble."

Still, there was no response from the missing couple.

"Ned, sound long, short, long on the whistle." This was a signal for the group to meet. "We should get together and start a hunt for the fourth couple."

This was done, and in a few minutes Bess, Dave, Burt, and George had joined Ned and Nancy.

"What's up?" Burt asked.

"You didn't hear a fourth whistle, did you?" Nancy asked.

The two couples shook their heads.

"Then we must start a hunt for Wanna and Don."

They looked around until Nancy spied Don helping Wanna climb a steep incline.

"Are you all right?" Nancy called down. "You didn't answer our signal."

Wanna replied, "Sorry. We didn't hear it. But come down here. We have a wonderful surprise for you!"

CHAPTER XVIII

Surprise Gift

RELIEVED that the missing couple were all right, Nancy and her friends followed them down the rocky slope. At the foot of it was a deep recess.

"Here it is," said Wanna. She pulled out a package.

Nancy's eyes glistened. "Don't tell me——"

Wanna and Don smiled, and the young Indian woman said, "Yes it is—another one of the missing tablets. I'm sure."

She unwrapped the object, and Nancy looked at it eagerly.

"This certainly looks like the others," she said.

Taking her magnifying glass from a pocket, she trained it on the left- and right-hand corners of the stone tablet.

"This is one of the missing pieces, all right," she said. "Here's the chuckwalla in the left-hand corner, and in the right——" She stopped speaking.

The others waited for an explanation. Finally Bess asked, "Did you find something else?"

Nancy said she had a new theory about the markings in the right-hand corner. She had wondered all along if there were some ancient way of indicating the order in which the tablets should be placed to give a continuous story.

"This may be a wild theory," she said at last, "but I believe that the moon was used as a way of discerning how this puzzle worked. Seven phases could have been used. The new moon was number one. Number four was probably the full moon and five and six the waning moon."

Nancy's friends were used to her logical deductions, but Wanna and Don stared at the girl in amazement.

"That's very clever," Don remarked. "Which tablet do you think this one is?"

Nancy's guess was number three, the one just before the full moon.

"The mark on this part of each tablet is so faint, it's really difficult to decide what it was meant to be. But the petroglyphs the three tablets I've seen so far are similar to the way we picture phases of the moon."

Everyone in the group wondered if more of the tablets might be hidden in this niche in the rocks. They hunted inside it and all around the area. Finally they gave up, sure that there was nothing more in that particular spot.

"I wish we could find Mrs. Wabash's stolen dictionary," Nancy said.

"What do you make of this tablet?" Ned asked her.

She studied it for a minute, then replied, "Possibly it's the one right next to the tablet that wasn't stolen from Mrs. Wabash. As I recall, that one had a full circle pictured on it, which could mean the full moon.

"A large group of people definitely trekked into this area and settled here. Then something happened and many of them died. Perhaps it was a war or a drought or some epidemic."

"But they didn't all die," Bess spoke up.

"I think not," Nancy replied, "but they probably fled from here."

She asked Don which of the four civilizations he thought had made the plaque.

"I believe every tablet will have to be carbondated to find out its age. The only thing certain is that all of them came from a peculiar sandstone type of rock in this area."

Dave noted that it was getting very hot. "And that means we should go back to camp and cool off."

Bess said she would be glad to get off her feet. "My ankle hurts a little," she admitted. "Maybe I won't join you this afternoon."

Nancy nodded. "It's a good idea. Why don't you spend most of the time lying down and reading?"

"I think I will."

They all returned to their cars and rode off. When they reached camp, the searchers found it buzzing with excitement. Many diggers had been lucky that morning, finding various artifacts. Now they proudly displayed them.

"Oh, see these beautiful shells!" Wanna remarked. "It's unusual to find them in the desert. I wonder if these could have been brought here from the coast by visiting or warring Indians."

Don had a different idea. "I am pretty well convinced that at one time what is now an underground river was aboveground. Wouldn't there have been all sorts of little creatures with shells in the water?"

Like so many of the questions that had been brought up in connection with the Forgotten City this one also had to go unanswered for the present.

Nancy and Ned had walked over to one of the Nevada students. He was proudly displaying an ancient pipe. It was cylindrical in shape and had a hole in the middle.

"Not a very interesting way to smoke," Ned remarked. He picked it up. "This weighs a ton!"

The student said he wondered just how the ancient Indians used the pipe. "I understand they didn't smoke for pleasure, just for ceremonials. When two warring factions finally declared a truce, the elders of the tribe would gather around a pile of burning tobacco. Then each man would suck the smoke up through the stem of his own pipe."

Nancy recalled having heard that later generations of Indians had stopped wandering around as hunters and had become farmers.

"This gave them more leisure time, and they developed religious customs. The men had secret meetings down in great pits, which were called *kivas*. Smoking was part of their ceremonies."

As the campers were finishing their midday meal, someone called out, "Visitors for Nancy Drew!"

Nancy was surprised. Who could be calling on her? She hurried outside the tent. One of the Nevada girls pointed to a car standing nearby.

"There they are," she said.

Nancy walked over to it. The car was large and flashy. The couple inside were gaudily dressed, which seemed out of place in this desert landscape.

"You're Nancy Drew?" the man asked. When she nodded, he went on, "We're Mr. and Mrs. Horace Greene from Los Angeles. We've been spending a little time in Las Vegas and——"

His wife interrupted. "Nancy, it's very hot out

there. Please get into the back seat, where it's cool, so we can talk to you."

Nancy climbed in. The car was cool. It made her sneeze several times.

"Oh, I'm sorry," said Mrs. Greene. "Horace and I don't mind the cold, but we positively cannot stand the heat!"

Nancy wondered who the couple were. Beyond the fact that they evidently had a great deal of money, she could not figure out anything about them.

Mr. Greene seemed inclined to talk about the heat, the long drive, and his annoyance that he could not play golf.

Finally his wife interrupted him. "Why don't you show Miss Drew what you came here to talk to her about?"

"Oh yes, yes," he said. "Well, a man walked into our hotel. He said he was from the University of Nevada Museum. They had too many artifacts there and he had been given special permission to sell some of them."

Mr. Greene paused and began to unwrap a box that lay on the front seat between the couple.

Mrs. Greene turned around to face Nancy. "Horace paid a horribly big sum of money for this thing. But we just felt we couldn't pass it up."

By this time her husband had the box open.

He unwrapped the object inside. Nancy stared at it in astonishment.

Another one of the missing tablets!

"Queer looking, isn't it?" Mr. Greene asked Nancy. "We drove over to the Lost City Museum to find out what it said. The curator there couldn't tell us much, but he suggested that we come out here and find you. My, you look so young, Miss Drew. Are you a special student in this kind of work?"

Nancy took the tablet and looked at it carefully. There was no doubt in her mind but that this was one of the original collection of six stolen from Mrs. Wabash.

She looked up and asked, "You say that the man who sold this was from the University of Nevada museum?"

"That's what he said," Mrs. Greene replied. "The way you ask that question sounds as if you don't believe it."

"No, I don't," Nancy replied. "I'm sorry to have to say this, but you have purchased stolen property. It belongs to a woman I know."

"What!" Mrs. Greene shrieked.

Her husband asked, "How do you know this?"

Without going into too much detail, Nancy told the couple how she happened to become interested in the case and actually had helped to capture the thief, who was now in jail.

"I believe he's in Las Vegas. If you'd like me to, I can verify my story."

"Oh, I believe you," Mr. Greene said, "but I am shocked to think that I was taken in so easily."

Suddenly Mrs. Greene threw the box and papers onto the back seat with Nancy. "Horace, don't you have another thing to do with that! We've bought stolen property! We're liable!"

Nancy gathered that Mr. Greene was used to taking orders from his wife and that he would now follow her advice.

He said to Nancy, "You know who the rightful owner is. Will you please give this to her? We want nothing more to do with it. Please wrap this up and take it. We will drive off at once."

Nancy was stunned by the announcement, but she made no protest. Quickly she got out of the car, taking the tablet, the box, and the wrapping paper with her. Mr. Greene backed up, turned the car, and sped off across the desert.

Nancy stood looking after the Greenes. What an amazing way to receive stolen property! When she joined her friends and told them the story, they were perplexed.

"You're sure," George spoke up, "that this plaque is one of the set?"

Nancy laughed. "You think I might have been gypped and this is a clever copy? But remember, I didn't pay anything for it!"

After lunch Wanna and Don joined Nancy and her friends and gazed at the tablet. Nancy pointed out that it was almost entirely covered with wild animals, large and small, all the way from the giant sloth to the little chip fox.

She turned to Ned. "I think we should return our two tablets to Mrs. Wabash immediately. Want to go to town with me? And how about any one else?"

Burt and George decided to go. "You may need my judo protection in case of a holdup," George stated, grinning.

"We'll go in the daylight so it won't be so risky," Nancy replied. "But I'd love to have you along."

The four set off in Nancy's rented car. They reached Mrs. Wabash's house without incident at five o'clock. She was overjoyed to receive the tablets and kept reiterating how amazing the whole story was.

"You're going to so much trouble for me," she told the young people. "I never could repay you."

Nancy smiled. "Let's just say that if we can be of use to our country by uncovering the secrets of the past, that will be a great big reward for us."

"Oh bless you!" the Indian woman said. "I'm sure my ancestors did not want the history of the people here forgotten entirely. It was pure

"We've bought stolen property!" the woman shrieked.

luck that our paths crossed, but I am very happy about it."

"We all are," George assured her.

Mrs. Wabash insisted that the young people stay to dinner. They were very glad to and watched her prepare it. Later, after helping the woman tidy up, the visitors said they must leave.

Burt suggested that they park the car downtown and walk around a little. "I'd like to stretch and exercise after that big meal, and before our long trip back."

Ned left the car in a parking lot and took the key to the attendant.

As they walked along the main boulevard, he said, "Maybe I should go back and lock the car. I forgot to."

"Oh, don't bother," Nancy told him. "There's nothing in there worth stealing and we won't be gone long."

After covering several blocks, the group turned around and started back. When they reached the corner, they were held up by a red traffic light.

An instant later Burt said, "I really suspect we'd better go back. This tired man wants to go to the car. Please walk behind me, George."

Nancy and the others realized that this was a coded message, saying, "Suspect man behind."

The group turned so suddenly that they nearly knocked the man down. He balanced himself, then scooted off on the crowded sidewalk.

"Shall we follow him?" Ned asked Nancy.

"I doubt that it would do any good," she said. "But I did recognize him. He's one of the two men whose picture Dave snapped that night in the motel garden."

"I wonder why he's here," George asked. "I'll bet he's up to something!"

Burt laughed. "If he is, we've nipped his idea in the bud."

The two couples reached their car and climbed in. Again Ned took the wheel with Nancy alongside him.

They had gone less than a block when suddenly George from the rear seat cried out, "Nancy, there's a snake beside you!"

George made a lunge for the reptile just as its fangs were ready to strike her friend.

CHAPTER XIX

Nancy Disappears

As George grabbed the back of the snake's head with one hand, she opened the car door with the other.

"Stop! Stop!" she cried out.

Ned pulled up short, and instantly George got out. She had a good grip on the snake, which was wriggling and trying to free itself. The snake was not large but it whipped its tail up over her hand.

"Turn the flashlight on him!" she requested.

By this time Burt had climbed out of the car too. He held the light on the snake, which seemed to be confused by it and stopped wriggling.

"Want me to kill it?" Burt asked.

George looked disdainful. "Certainly not. This little creature is needed in the desert. If he weren't around, the place might be overrun with rodents."

162

"Okay, lady professor," Burt replied. "Now tell me what it is."

George admitted she was not sure, but thought it was a sidewinder. "I'll know when I put it down, but I'm not going to do so here in town. We'll take it out in the desert and let the poor thing loose."

Still grasping the reptile, she got back into the car, and once more Ned drove off. When they reached the turn to go into the desert road, George asked him to let her out once more.

Burt trained his flashlight on the snake as George set it down on the ground. The little creature seemed stupefied for a few seconds; then it began to move. The snake progressed by looping its body as it slithered away.

"It's a sidewinder all right," Burt remarked.

There was a discussion as to how the snake had gotten into the car. All four young people agreed it could not have crawled inside by itself.

"Someone put it here," Nancy declared. "But who?"

Ned recalled that he had not locked the car, so it would have been easy for anyone to open the door.

George said, "If someone at camp was playing a joke, it was a mean one. Do you think Archie could be responsible?"

"No," Nancy replied. "Archie's a nuisance but

he isn't bad. Besides, if the snake was in the car when we left camp, we would have seen it sooner."

Burt was more inclined to think that one of their enemies had done it. "Don't forget that man on the street. Nancy thought he was a buddy of Fleetfoot's."

"And he had plenty of time to put the snake in," Ned said. "He might have been watching us all the time and was following us back here, expecting to watch the fun."

Burt remarked that some people's idea of fun was warped. "Nancy, I'm glad you weren't bitten."

Ned had a new suggestion. "Suppose someone we don't know played this trick. The snake could have been in a torpid state and just revived in the parking lot."

When the four friends reached camp, they found Archie giving a dozen of the diggers a lecture on something he had found that afternoon. It was a small pottery bowl, which he had picked up in pieces but had mended nicely.

The bowl, an attractive one, was light tan in color and had a black swastika-like design on it. Archie claimed that this had come from the very earliest civilization of the Moapa Valley.

Nancy and the others joined Bess and Dave. After listening for a while, they looked at one another. All of them knew from their studies and from what they had seen in the museum that this bowl was not that old and probably had been dropped recently where Archie had found it.

"Everything around here is red in color," Nancy whispered to her friends. "Later civilizations of Indians far to the south of us had the tan clay, but there is none of it in this area."

She and her friends decided not to spoil Archie's lecture. As usual he was being eloquent and pompous and having a very good time.

Ned whispered, "I'm sure his listeners will find out the truth sooner or later, so let him have fun."

Nancy and her friends walked off and she said, "Well good night everybody. See you in the morning. I can't wait to get out to the Valley of Fire again to make another search."

By four the next morning the searchers were on their way. When they reached the spot where they always left their car, they were startled to find another automobile there. Mrs. Wabash stepped out.

"What a wonderful surprise!" Nancy said, running up to the Indian woman. "Good morning!"

Mrs. Wabash greeted everyone, then said, "I have some very exciting news for you that you won't believe!"

"Fleetfoot didn't escape, did he?" Burt asked.

"No, that's not my news." The Indian woman smiled. "What I have to tell you is what you call a bombshell. The police found out where Fleet-foot had been living. In a closet in his bedroom behind his clothes, they found my missing petro-glyph dictionary!"

"How wonderful!" Nancy exclaimed. "Now we can decipher what's on the four stone tablets we have, and get a connected story."

Again Mrs. Wabash smiled. "I have not told you all my news," she said quietly. "Crayoned onto the walls of his closet, Fleetfoot had put marks. When the police took me there, I thought at once they might indicate places where Fleet-foot had hidden the rest of the tablets."

"Do you remember what the marks were?" Nancy asked.

Mrs. Wabash said she had not trusted her memory. She had asked the police to take a photo-graph of the marks. She opened her purse. "Here is a copy." She handed it to Nancy.

The girl detective took it eagerly and looked at the various marks.

Suddenly she exclaimed excitedly, "I'm sure this one indicates the place where Wanna and Don found one of the tablets."

"Which just about proves," George said, "that the other marks are the rest of Fleetfoot's hiding places. Let's start our search!"

Mrs. Wabash said that she did not feel equal to climbing around the rocks. "I'll wait for you here. With the hope that you find the rest of the tablets, I brought along the ones I have. I also have some magazines to read. I'll be all right. Don't worry about me."

The young people decided to divide their forces. Wanna stayed with Nancy and Ned. The other two couples each chose one of the other places to hunt. Again it was arranged for them to use whistles at fifteen-minute intervals to signify that everyone was all right.

"Let's change our signaling a little," Nancy suggested. "If you're just telling us you're all right, give one long blast. If you find a tablet, give two blasts. If you find two, use your whistle three times."

"This arithmetic is too much for me," Bess said. "Dave, you remember it."

The group separated and climbed to their various positions. Nancy, Ned, and Wanna had gone to a rock that looked like a poodle lying down. They hunted assiduously all around the stone animal but found nothing.

Nearly twenty minutes had gone by, and Nancy felt she should start signaling. She blew one long blast on her whistle. A few seconds later George and Burt replied with one blast. Several seconds went by. Then, to everyone's delight, they heard the third whistle give two long distinct blasts.

"That's Bess and Dave!" Nancy said. "They've found a tablet."

She assumed that the couple would return to Mrs. Wabash's car. Burt and George and her own group would continue to search.

Wanna sighed. "Maybe there's more than one poodle around here," she said.

With this thought in mind, the three searchers spread out a little and began hunting for another rock formation that resembled the poodle. None of them found one and they were puzzled.

Nancy sat down on a somewhat flat rock to think. "What does a poodle resemble?" she asked herself.

Wanna and Ned came to the girl's side, and she asked them the same question. While each of them was trying to form a picture in his mind, Nancy realized that it was time for her to blow the whistle again. She gave a loud blast on it, then waited.

The answering signal soon came. To her delight there were two shrill responses.

"George and Burt have found a tablet!" she announced. "Fleetfoot's directions were perfect!"

Wanna and Ned looked at her and he said, "So we get the booby prize. What's the matter with us?"

In a flash the answer came to Nancy. "A poodle

that hasn't been clipped could look like a baby mountain lamb that has no horns yet."

"You're right!" Ned exclaimed. "And there's one looking right at me."

He climbed to a stone figure that had one paw lifted. Under it was the tablet!

Nancy and Wanna quickly joined him and examined the stone plaque.

"It's one of them all right!" the young Indian student said gleefully.

Nancy checked it with her magnifying glass. "Yes," she agreed, "and here is another phase of the moon pictured."

"I'm glad the hunt is over," Ned said. "I'm tired of hunting for wild animals that aren't real."

The three successful searchers hurried down to Mrs. Wabash's car, Ned waving the plaque in the air.

"You found the last one!" the woman exclaimed. "How wonderful!"

Nancy's friends were already there and had handed over the tablets they had found.

Tears formed in the Indian woman's eyes. "I can't believe it!" she exclaimed. "Oh you dear, dear people!"

Ned, who disliked tears, said, "Let's try to arrange these stones in order, Mrs. Wabash. With the help of your dictionary we'll see if we can piece out the full story about your ancestors and the Forgotten City."

Everyone helped. With the aid of Nancy's magnifying glass, they were able to accomplish this by putting the tablets containing the phases of the moon in the correct order.

Mrs. Wabash looked at the figures and kept consulting her paper, figuring out the probable translation of the petroglyphs.

After a while she heaved a sigh. "A complete analysis of this is going to take some time," she said. "As I see it now, one man centuries ago pictured the world of his day. It included life along the Muddy River and the finding of gold. He had gathered many nuggets and fashioned a series of gold plates. An enemy tribe came, so he hid them.

"Unfortunately I can't see that he told where they were," Mrs. Wabash remarked. "It also says here that he had made other matching tablets on which future generations were to write their history."

"One thing that puzzles me," said Nancy, "is why you call these different tribes your ancestors, Mrs. Wabash."

The Indian woman said she figured that whenever a conquering tribe took over, there was intermarriage and part of her family had remained near the site of the Forgotten City.

"I wonder what its real name is," she mused.

Since it was becoming hot, Mrs. Wabash said she thought she would go home. The young people felt that the Indian woman should not travel without an escort. Nancy suggested that they all go to the camp. From there the boys would follow her home.

"You're very kind," Mrs. Wabash said. "I will accept your offer, since I will be carrying such a precious load in my car."

As soon as the girls were left at the camp, Nancy sought out Don. He had just returned from his dig. She told him of their unusual good fortune during the morning's expedition.

"Magnificent!" he said. "When the story becomes known, what a buzz there will be in the scientific world!"

It was hard for Nancy to relax during the hottest hours of the day. Having solved part of the mystery, she was eager to go on a further hunt for the plates of gold. At four o'clock her group was ready to start out again.

When they reached the deep hole that led down to the water, she said, "This time I'd like to go down."

"Okay, but take it easy," Ned warned.

An underarm sling was put over Nancy and the ropes lowered.

"Don't stay long," said Bess, who was fearful about Nancy's going at all.

When the young sleuth reached the bottom,

she spotted an object in the wall of the watery tunnel opposite her. Wondering what it was, she tried to reach across. This was impossible.

"I guess the only way I can get there is to let myself out of this sling and reach over," she told herself, and slipped from the ropes.

Nancy was in the midst of wading across, when there was a rush of water through the tunnel toward her. It knocked the girl over, and the current swept her along into the foaming tunnel.

Nancy never panicked, but now she knew she was in serious trouble. If the tunnel remained as wide as it was, she might be carried outside and be able to save herself.

"But if the passageway gets too narrow to carry me through——" she thought. Nancy closed her eyes and prayed.

CHAPTER XX

A Fagot of Treasure

At the topside, Ned and the others waited for Nancy to tug the rope. Nothing happened. Ten more minutes went by and still there was no signal.

Finally Ned called down, "Are you ready, Nancy?"

There was no answer.

"Are you sure she can hear you?" George asked, alarm showing on her face.

Ned got down on his knees, leaned over the hole, and shouted at the top of his lungs.

"Nancy! Nancy!"

The only reply was the hollow echo of his own voice.

"Oh I know something dreadful has happened to her!" Bess wailed. "What are we going to do?"

Ned was grim. He tugged the rope and realized there was nothing on the end of it.

"She's not there!" he announced.

Hoping Nancy had gone adventuring and sent up a note to explain, he pulled up the rope quickly. No note was attached. By this time everyone was frantic, and Bess was crying.

Ned tried to remain calm but was tense. "Nancy got out of this sling deliberately," he stated. "I'm going down there to find her! If I have any information, I'll send up a note."

He fastened himself into the harness, and the others let the rope down. When he reached the bottom, Ned looked up and down the tunnel. Nancy was nowhere in sight.

"Nancy! Nancy!" he called.

He repeated her name over and over. There was no sound except the rushing water.

"I must go after her," he thought, determined.

Ned wondered, however, which way to go. He decided that there was little likelihood that she had battled against the stream.

"She must have gone downstream," he decided.

Before getting out of the sling, Ned pulled a notebook and pencil from a pocket and wrote a message to the watchers above. It said:

Nancy not here. Does not answer. Going downstream to try to find her. Suggest two of you go to water hole and dig tunnel in case she's stuck.

Ned took off the harness, attached the note to

it, then tugged on the rope. Quickly it was pulled up and the note read.

"We'll follow instructions," Burt called down. "George and I will go over to the waterhole. The others can stay here in case you send up more notes." They let the rope down again.

George and Burt grabbed picks and shovels and raced off. When they reached the spring, the two started digging furiously to enlarge the hole. Soon a larger flow of water was coming into the water hole.

Meanwhile Nancy had been swept along the tunnel. She had managed to keep her flashlight on and kept looking for a place where she could stop or find something she could cling to. At first she found nothing, and went on. The tunnel curved and was so narrow at times that she had to duck under the water to avoid being hit.

"I mustn't drown!" she kept telling herself.

Presently the tunnel widened and the roof sloped upward again. Her flashlight revealed a large square niche on one side. It was slightly above water level, and the young detective managed to drag herself up into it. To her delight and relief, the opening was high enough so she could stand up straight.

"Thank goodness!" she murmured.

Instead of wondering how she was going to get back, Nancy beamed her flashlight around the opening.

"What are these?"

At the back of the opening was a smaller niche, which formed a sort of shelf.

"Something's lying on it!" Nancy thought, excited.

A couple of steps brought her to the spot. On it lay a bundle made of tightly woven twigs. Nancy lifted the fagot. It was small, but very heavy.

Just as the girl detective was speculating breathlessly on whether or not the fagot contained the missing plates of gold, Ned swam up to her.

"Nancy! Nancy! How relieved I am to see you!" he exclaimed, pulling himself out of the water and standing beside her. "Are you all right? Why did you come here alone?"

She told him what had happened, and he frowned. "A rush of water! That could happen again. We'd better get out of here!"

"Not yet, Ned," she pleaded as she looked at her friend fondly. "I'm terribly glad you came. I think perhaps I've made a great discovery." She pointed to the bundle on the shelf. "This may be the lost treasure of the Forgotten City!"

Ned's mind was still on the danger they were in. "Treasure or no treasure, do you realize what can happen to us if the water rises?"

Nancy realized that he had risked his life to save her. "You're right, Ned, but just give me half a minute. I do want to take that bundle with us. Then we'll get back somehow."

Ned told her that George and Burt were probably working frantically at the spot where the underground river came out through the bottom of the water hole, which was rather shallow.

"Listen!" he said tensely. "Do you hear a sound like digging?"

Nancy's face lit up. "I certainly do. And it doesn't seem far away."

Hand-in-hand the couple waited expectantly. Presently they could hear voices.

"We're saved!" Nancy said. "Your idea was an inspiration, Ned."

Within minutes there was a breakthrough and the hole was large enough for Nancy and Ned to swim to their friends.

"Let's go!" he said eagerly.

"Can you possibly take this package?" Nancy asked, handing it to him.

Ned lifted the fagot to his shoulders and held it there with one hand. Now he and Nancy let themselves back into the water, and he swam with one hand. Seconds later, the couple were swept out to the water hole.

"Thank goodness you two are all right!" George cried out.

Burt, mud spattered but grinning said, "What an experience!"

"I confess," said Nancy, "that for a while I was scared. Thank you. Thank you a million."

Burt asked, "Ned, what's in that fagot on your shoulder?"

"We don't know yet," Nancy answered. "But I'm wishing it's the lost treasure of the Forgotten City."

"You mean the gold plates?" George asked skeptically.

Nancy nodded. "I'm hoping my guess is right, and that we won't all be fooled."

At this moment Wanna joined the group.

"Nancy," she said, "we were dreadfully worried about you and Ned. I'm so happy to see you're safe. Tell us what happened. And how did you get here?"

Nancy pointed to their escape route.

Wanna surveyed the large opening of the underground river and cried out with joy. "My theory has been proved!"

The others nodded. Ned smiled. "This should get you an extra college degree!"

Wanna smiled. "But I shall have to give all the credit to Nancy Drew."

"No, indeed," Nancy objected. "Everyone in our special group had a hand in this whole exciting adventure."

Wanna said she would summon Bess and Dave to join them. She blew a loud blast on her

whistle. Within minutes the other couple arrived. Bess hugged Nancy and cried a little.

"It's so wonderful to see you alive and okay!"
she said.

Burt explained about the opening through
which the underground river flowed. He said this
no doubt would help speed the curator's dream
that this would become a lush area in the desert.
"Once more it can be a great farming spot for
the Indians."

"Let's open the bundle!" Ned suggested. "I
want to find out whether that golden treasure
is really in it."

Unwinding the interlaced twigs was a tedious
job. The whole group of young archaeologists
realized that even the covering was valuable for
historical purposes.

"This was certainly ingeniously woven,"
George remarked.

"And it's amazing," Wanna added, "that it is
in such good shape. It's my guess that these twigs
came from bushes by the Muddy River and the
dampness inside the tunnel was like food for
them."

Finally the outer covering came off in one
piece. Underneath were several layers of bark.
These were carefully removed.

When the contents of the bundle were finally
revealed, everyone stared in amazement. There

were four oblong plates of gold. They were in perfect condition and all were covered with fine-lined symbols. Had they been done with a stone or some sharp-pointed instrument? The answer would take a lot of study.

"The story of the golden treasure is true!" Bess burst out. "And Nancy and Ned risked their lives to find it!"

At camp that night, Nancy found a few minutes to be alone. The usual feeling of emptiness came over her whenever she had solved a mystery. She longed for another, that came as *The Sky Phantom*.

People at the camp had been hurriedly summoned by telephone. Mrs. Wabash drove out. The curator, his wife, and their daughter were there along with several State Police to guard the valuable find. Now the whole story was told to the group of young archaeologists.

Professor Don Maguire got up to speak. "Everyone on this dig has made a valuable contribution to science," he said, "but I think we should have a rousing cheer for Nancy Drew. Her discovery is invaluable!"

Nancy blushed at the applause and calls that filled the desert air.